Neighborhood Ties

By: Neil Mena

ISBN-9798751509507

We Helped This Author Self-Publish This Book
And We Can Also Help You Too
Contact -Crystell Publications
PO BOX 8044 / Edmond – OK 73083
www.crystellpublications.com
(405) 414-3991

Printed in the USA

Neighborhood Ties

ACKNOWLEDGEMENTS

This part right here had me thinking a lot. There are so many people that motivated me, supported me, and assisted me with this project.

Let me start off by thanking the most highest for blessing me with the ability to write and providing me the opportunity to do so. My grandmother (R.I.P.) Yia-Ya would be so proud if she could witness this.

This lane right here is paving a foundation for my kids. What's up Elijah, Maliyah and Prince? Your pops handled the business with this novel. I love you all to death!

I told you mom that I could be successful in other areas besides the streets. My baby mother Saran, this time around I will remain out there to raise our children. I salute you to the fullest for doing it solo while I've been absent. I will forever hold you down. We are family for life regardless! Shout out to my little brother Adam, my aunt Gigi, my uncle Jerry, and my cousins Gabi, Danny, Monique, Kevin, Nico, and C.J. Love y'all!

To my wife Melissa Mena. You have been a pillar of strength, vision and guidance for me during my incarceration. I sit back and marvel at the sequence of events that has brought us this close. We have been building solid blocks necessary to uphold a firm foundation that will never crack or break. I appreciate your sacrifice and inconveniences. You have enriched my life and I love you deeply for that! I thank you Melissa. This is another step forward in our long journey that lies ahead.

Last but not least, shout out to all my comrades. Y'all been real with ya boy and I do this for all of us. Truth, Blanco, Link, Legacy, Kane, Eckz, Wolf, Bonez, Nino, Lo, Rell, Reemo, Lady Smilez, Johnny Kash , Tru, PZ, Kode Red, Infamous, Dub G, Fat E, Philly Whop, Lil Smilez, Itchy, K.I, BD, J. Gutta, King, Junebug, Kuncklez, Shady, Twinz, Haze, Bath, CK, Antonio, A.R., JoJo Skrap, Princess, and Kream. Also, Free-the-Doves, L-Farmer, Kaliko, Murda, Big Moe, Blackface, X, Red Hoodie, Bash Gatez, Big Loko, Baby Bomb, Big O-Dog, Gash, Rated-R.

My bad if I ain't name you, there's so many people I'm doing this off my memory

Also shout out to Real Rights I met along my travels: Stuffy (ROC), Tye Payso (BSV), Jem Ru (TTP), Trent (Niagara Falls), Kenny (D.C.), The Loc Shorty Mac (30's), Tim (60's), Knock (CPP), Salty (I.F.), Red Riding Hood (CMB), Ty Gunz (BSV), S.I. (NTG), Whoodini (183), C.B. (SMM), Milk (AGC), Pebbs (YG), Mac 11 (SMM), Mass (Double I), G-Bam (GMB), Antonio (D.C.), Buck (BRL), Lil Man (G.D.), Solo (BPS), Kaos (JSB), D (NHB), Hov (111 Payback), C-Blaze (Grape St.), Mitch (West B-More), Prince (SMM), Black (Buffalo), Sparxx (NHB), J-Boogs (SMM), Streets (Pittsburgh), Wood (Detroit), Frag (8Trey), Mark Reiter (Harlem), Hollywood (Pittsburgh), Gotti (Latin Folk), B (Lancaster PA), Y-B (Makk), Dutch

(NTG), Cheese (BX), Payroll (Makk), Ackman (Philly), Dame (ROC), J.K. (Hound), Weezy (Beven), Chino (NHB), Abu (D.C.), G-Baby (BSGG), D.J. (N.C.), and Dave (N.J.).

I apologize for those I didn't mention. So many names and so many. official people I met through my travels. I appreciate all y'all love and support. I'm getting a different kind of money now - legit paper! Two things that motivated me were my family and all the haters.

Be on the lookout for part two. Tell a friend to tell a friend.

INTRODUCTION

It was a hot summer day in the Bronx. The Park was filled with children running under sprinklers, barely clothed women flirting, and local hustlers sporting their newest pieces of jewelry. The air was thick with the smell of charcoal and barbeque. The young and the old were sitting around the park enjoying the freshly cooked ribs, chicken, and burgers.

"Ayo Razor," Krazy shouted. "There goes the young cat you were looking for right there." Krazy pointed to a group of young teenagers shooting hoops in the basketball court.

Razor nodded and strolled into the park along with six other O.G.'s from the neighborhood. As the crew approached the crowd of teenagers to check on their young prospect, they parted like the Rea Sea out of respect.

"That ain't Red, Krazy. You gotta get your eyes checked out, fool!" Razor shook his head side to side and looked around aggressively. "Where is Red at? Anyone know his whereabouts?"

A skinny teen with an oversized white t-shirt pointed to a wooded area behind the courts. "He's back there with Crystal."

Razor gestured to three of his newest recruits. "Y'all go back there and whoop Red's ass. He may run the playground, but he ain't blood until we say he blood on the "B". Go handle that."

The three soldiers immediately left to carry out the order. Within two minutes, they had spotted their target. Red was sitting on a bench with his head leaned back, currently enjoying the pleasure of Crystal's warm mouth and tongue ring sliding up and down on his manhood.

At the sound of boots on gravel, Red snapped out of his trance. He looked up and saw the three bloods charging at him. In one quick motion, Red pulled up his sweatpants with his left hand while pushing Crystal's head from his lap with his right. Before he could put his hands up to defend himself, one of the bloods sidelined him in the jaw.

A rush of adrenaline shot into Red. He was only 15 years old but had been fighting all of his life. He shrugged off the first blow and immediately launched himself into the fight.

"One blood, two blood, three blood, four blood..." was all that could be heard from Razor as a crowd of people formed around the fight. Razor had never had the chance to see Red perform like this. He had heard stories and rumors about the young prospect, but was about to witness it first-hand.

Red getting jumped was nothing out of the ordinary. As he embraced each blow, he returned a flurry of jabs, hooks, and power rights. It was obvious to all that watched that Red's days at P.A.L. Boxing had honed his fighting skills. Within seconds, two of the three assailants were on the ground, out of the fight. Red might have been young, but his body was sculpted from all the burpees, push-ups, and pull-ups he did at all of the different juvenile facilities.

Red and the last soldier exchanged blows and went toe-to-toe for about a minute before both heard Razor yell.

"A'ight, that's it. Break that shit up now." Razor's muscular arms were crossed across his huge chest, and he was smiling despite himself. Red's performance had impressed him.

Red wiped the blood dripping from his busted lip with the bottom of his burgundy t-shirt. He looked around the crowd and made eye contact with a few familiar faces. Eventually his eyes locked with the big homie, the man he idolized. Razor had taught him everything he knew.

"Yo lil homie - today you proved you're worthy enough to be an official member of Neighborhood Gangstas." Razor walked up to Red and handed him a brand-new red bandana. He was still smiling at his protege.

Red looked up at Razor with a serious expression on his face. "Yo on Neighborhood I won't let you down. I will represent us with loyalty, pride, and honor till the death of me."

Razor looked back and nodded his head up and down. He realized he had created a monster in these streets.

* * *

Razor was a reputable member of the notorious Neighborhood Gangstas, a blood chapter that was founded in South Central Los Angeles. After the last war with their rivals, Harlem 30s, things got real hectic in his hood and Razor decided to migrate from California to New York along with a few of his comrades.

After leaving Cali, Razor tried living in a few other states. He liked Texas, Florida, and New Jersey, but New York just felt like home. Even with the police harassing him, enemies lurking around, and close friends dying, he was amazed at the city that never sleeps. It was a big transition for him, but Razor fell in love with the Big Apple.

Razor moved to the Parkchester section of the Bronx when he first arrived in the city. Within days, he had met a beautiful Puerto Rican woman named Jennifer. She managed to hold his eyes hostage longer than usual and was the most elegant woman he had ever met. Jennifer was 5'5", had a pale complexion, long red hair that hung to her mid-back, green eyes, and a body that other women would die for.

After being formally introduced by a mutual friend, Razor and Jennifer started dating. After only a few months of being a couple, their relationship began to truly grow. They found they had so much in common with each other and it was easy to talk.

Jennifer was a little hesitant at first to introduce Razor to her only child, but that feeling quickly faded. The only other man Nelson had ever known was his father who passed away when he was six from stage four lung cancer.

When Razor finally met Nelson, AKA Red, he instantly took a liking to him. Razor saw so much of himself in the youngster. He had never had any real serious relationships before since all of his time, effort, and energy was dedicated to the hood. He had never had any kids of his own before, and now had a woman and a son in his life. This was a big challenge for him.

Razor tried numerous times to steer Red away from the street life that had sucked him in and made him a slave to the gang world. He knew well the consequences and repercussions of that gang culture. He had done time in

California prisons from Pelican Bay to Soledad during his 10-year incarceration. A plea on a shooting charge led to being locked away in some of the most vicious prisons in the country for a decade.

Razor didn't want Red to have the same life that he had gone through. He had many long talks and explained his experience with the street life. Unfortunately, Red continuously managed to find trouble.

Red started off doing little petty crimes but later graduated to dealing narcotics. That eventually landed him into a juvenile facility, Brookwood Secure Center, in Claverack, New York for three years.

Since Razor couldn't guide Red off the path of destruction, he chose to school him on the rules to the game he was playing. When Red came home from Brookwood, he mimicked Razor to the fullest. He wore red clothes every day, rocked red bandanas, and used all of the slang from L.A.'s gang culture. All of this led up to Red's initiation to the bloods. This was the life Red wanted, so this was the life he was going to live.

CHAPTER 1

SIX YEARS LATER

- Shut the fuck up!" Red said. He glanced back and forth from his red G-Shock watch to the hundred-or-so Neighborhood Gangstas crowded in front of him. "Razor is about to call my phone and talk to all of us."

It was late autumn, and red hoodies and skullys could be seen everywhere. The air was thick with the sound of bloods talking quietly to one another. Every month the set had these meetings. It was the perfect time to take Razor's call. Ever since the feds indicted Razor and Krazy for some armored truck heists, Red had put the Neighborhood Gangstas on his back.

- RING - RING - RING -

Red answered the phone and put it on speaker. "You have a pre-paid call. You will not be charged for this call. This call is from "Razor", an inmate at a federal prison. To accept this call, press 5. To block this call, press 7. To decline this call, hang up.

Red pressed 5 as soon as the recording ended.

"What up blood?" Razor said. "You around everybody yet or what?"

"Yeah, big bro, we all together already. Speak your piece."

Razor cleared his throat. "Salutations are extended to each and every one of y'all. This phone call is in reference to the letter I wrote to Red which he will show to you in a moment. Everything in there is valid and I want y'all to do what I said. Keep our movement solid and pure out there. Much love and much respect, Neighborhood G's till the pine box." His voice reached a scream before hanging up the phone.

A hush fell over the crowd, like they were in a courtroom awaiting the jury's decision. Red could tell from everyone's facial expressions that all were anxious to hear Razor's words.

Red reached into his back pocket and pulled out the letter Razor had written. "Just to clear up all the curiosity in the air, let me just read this kite." He looked up at the crowd one more time before beginning to read it aloud.

Dear Family,

I pray that with the arrival of this missive all of y'all remain focused and striving to the brink of greatness. Everyone should already know my current situation, but for those who don't, I will say this: these Feds put my lights out! They gave me 600 months, which is 50 years. I'm already 45 years old, so that's life for me. I need each and every one of y'all to trust my judgment on this. I'm giving Red the set now.

This is not up for debate. I taught him everything I know and raised him as my very own son. He eats, breathes, and sleeps Neighborhood. Red will take y'all in a direction that I haven't been able to. With my limited guidance from in here, things will prosper in everybody's benefit.

How can a person claim Neighborhood without protecting, investing, and uplifting their own neighborhood? Always remember that money is our number one motivation. Money is the number one element of power.

True brotherhood cannot exist in the shadow of ignorance. To birth greatness within we must be willing to see the world with a new pair of eyes. Endurance is not just the ability to bear a hard thing, but also to turn it into glory. At this point in time, I will be living through all y'all out there and your pictures, phone calls, visits, and e-mails.

Always know if you really want something you have to work for it. If you work for it, it will work for you in due time. I'm just a grain of sand in the midst of so many others to make a beach. B's up and know it's neighborhood gang or don't bang!

I remain, Infamous Razor

As Red spoke the last words of the letter, the crowd of Neighborhood homies went ballistic. "Soo Woo, Soo Woo!" was all you heard echoing through Cortona Park. Razor's letter ignited energy and emotions from his fellow comrades. His influential character had always had that effect on his set.

Red slowly took a step forward and stared at the crowd. "So does anyone challenge what the big homie said about the new leadership?" His eyes grilled the crowd, scanning for dissent. The park immediately grew quiet - so quiet that you could have heard a mouse pissing on cotton.

Most of the homies at the meeting had always been behind Red for years. Red had it embedded in his mind that leadership was a potent combination of both strategy and character. It just so happened that those were two traits Red prided himself in having. Once he became an official member of Neighborhood Gangtas bas he went all out for the set. Leading was something that came naturally to Red.

CHAPTER 2

It was a bright, sunny day outside, but it was clear that fall had arrived by the way the brisk wind blew dry, brown leaves around the block. Red puffed on a blunt of OG Kush in his apartment and stared out the window of his living room. Ever since he got the responsibility of being the top dog for his set, his mind had been wandering all over the place. Red knew that every move he made had to have purpose and direction. He could no longer just think with a selfish mentality, he had to make decisions for a collective whole.

As Red inhaled the kush, he watched out the window to see what was going on in his hood. On days like this, anything out of place caught his eye. Looking both up and down the block, he settled on a black Chevy Tahoe that was double-parked directly in front of his building. Red was born and raised in the hood.

He knew each and everybody that lived here and the cars they drove. This particular day there wasn't much activity around, and this car clearly did not belong.

Red lived on the third floor, and the fully tinted windows prevented him from seeing who the driver was. As the passenger-side window slid down, all you could hear was Jadakiss' raspy voice blaring through the speakers.

"Money, Power, Respect!" Red stared at the window and noticed a light skinned woman with long, black hair and sunglasses looking up at him.

Red didn't recognize the truck or the woman. He walked over to his bed and retrieved his loaded .357 from under the mattress. As he grabbed the black rubber grip, he kissed the side of the chrome barrel and shoved it into the waistband of his Nike sweats as he exited the apartment.

Red jogged down three flights of stairs and left the building. The black Tahoe was still parked out front and the music was turned all the way up.

He glanced to his left and right to make sure the coast was clear before drawing the .357 and training it on the truck. Red crept slowly towards the driver's side door and clutched the grip of the gun tighter as he drew close. Quickly, he snatched open the door in one fast motion with his left hand, keeping the gun raised with his right. Luckily, the door was unlocked.

Red pointed the barrel of the gun at the driver and heard a shrill cry from the female passenger.

"Yo what the fuck you doing blood? You lost your mind Skrap?" Bandz grabbed at the fallen Big Mac that had fallen onto his lap.

"Beloved why you parked in front of my building in this unfamiliar whip? Better yet, why you ain't call and notify me you were pulling up?" Red put down his gun, but kept the corners of his mouth tight.

"I called you about 50 times bro. You ain't pick up - check your jack." Bandz looked towards his female passenger to confirm what he had just told Red. "You forgot today is the day for that lick at the gambling spot?" Bandz pulled out his Android, pressed a few buttons, then passed the phone to Red.

"Yo that's how the spot looks. I snapped a picture to see if you seen it before." Bandz had a goofy smile on his face and waited for Red.

* * *

Red had known Bandz since they were both little kids. They did everything together: playing with GI-Joes, throwing rocks at cars, and gang banging.

The incident that forever bonded the two happened in the fifth grade.

Bandz was getting picked on by a bully named,

Dirty. He used to take Bandz' lunch money, punch him, and call him names. One day Red found out and beat up Dirty in the schoolyard in front of everyone.

Dirty was so embarrassed by that ass whooping that he eventually transferred to a new school. It wasn't that Bandz was soft, it's just that he was unaware of the gangsta that lied within him.

It didn't take long to see that Bandz would do anything for Red. As time progressed, Red tested Bandz on many different occasions. It was then that Bandz proved to Red he could uphold himself as a G in any situation. Not only did the two grow closer, Red also had much more respect for his friend.

* * *

"Damn Red - when are these white people gonna close up this spot so we can handle the business? I'm hungry as hell." Bandz took a bite out of a giant Snickers bar in his hand.

"Nigga you always hungry - that ain't nothing new. That's why your ass 300 pounds now."

Bandz looked up. "The door is opening - come on" He pulled out his 9-millimeter and ran out of the truck.

Red and Bandz crept up to the open door, dressed in all black. They had been waiting for the older white man to take out the garbage bags as he did every evening. As the man threw the last of the bags in the dumpster, Red pressed his .50 cal Desert Eagle to his temple.

"Ayo how much money y'all made at the gambling spot tonight?" Red clenched his teeth as he spoke to mask his voice.

"Not much, not much." The man stood still, but his voice trembled as he spoke.

Bandz cocked his 9 and pistol whipped the old man in the face until blood began to squirt from his mouth and forehead. Red grabbed him by the back collar of his shirt and dragged him down the stairs.

When they reached a long corridor, they could hear laughter and loud house music, along with the smell of expensive cigars. Red pushed open the door at the end of the hall and shoved the man on the floor. Before anyone could say anything, Bandz shot him in the back of the head, killing him instantly.

The loud bang of the gun got everyone's attention. Someone cut the music and it grew deathly quiet. "Nobody fucking move!" Red screamed through the black ski mask he wore. "Y'all already know what this is. Nobody else dies as long as you comply."

A blonde woman in her mid-40's stepped forward. "Okay, okay, you can have the money. My husband is going to be mad about this. Follow me back here."

At the same time, another woman ran towards the old man's lifeless body. She fell to her knees and began to cry hysterically as she caressed his face. The woman had to be in her 20's, had long blonde hair, and blue eyes. Shorty was flawless. "You fucking bastards you killed my father! How could you do this? He never hurt nobody!"

Red gripped his gun tight and did not respond to the woman. He didn't know why Bandz had shot the old man dead, but what's done is done."

The older woman stepped forward and put a calming hand on the other's shoulder. "Calm down Amber, it will be alright. I promise you."

Red stared at the woman. "Come on lady, let's go get this money now." The woman nodded and led Red to a large safe in the back room. It was wedged between a pool table, a large oak desk, and a beautiful fish tank. Because it was four in the morning, the spot was mostly empty. Bandz stood guard at the door anyway to make sure no one got in or out.

The older lady kept turning the combination. lock around but still hadn't opened it. "Hurry the fuck up lady," Red said. He knew it was Friday night and the gambling spot was loaded with cash. Finally, she put in the correct combination for the safe and Red heard it click open. He pushed the lady out of the way and began swiping stacks of money into the Army fatigue duffle bag he had with him.

"Come on Skrap let's go! We been here way too long," Bandz yelled from the other room.

Just then Red emerged with the duffle in one hand and the Desert Eagle in the other. "We out."

The two sprinted down the long corridor to exit the building.

- BLOCKA - BLOCKA - BLOCKA -

Bullets whizzed by Red and Bandz as they ran up the stairs and back out the door. Luckily they made it outside and down the block to their truck without getting hit by a single bullet. Bandz' shorty Amina was already in the driver's seat waiting to drive them away from the crime scene.

As they drove away, everyone was elated that no one had gotten locked up. They were lucky to be free and alive. Things definitely could have gone worse.

"This is $55,000 in total blood. I counted the money six times already." Bandz started to put the piles in stacks of five gees on the dining room table while Red sat on the black leather sofa.

Red sipped on a hundred-dollar bottle of Patron deep in thought. He almost didn't hear Bandz because so much weighed on his mind.

- RING - RING - RING -

Not even bothering to look down at the screen of his phone, Red answered. "Who is this?"

"It's me. GoGetta. I need your help ASAP Skrap."

"What you need lil bro?"

"I need you to bail me out. I got knocked out in Niagara County. It's only five thousand and I will get you the paper back." GoGetta sounded defeated.

"Aight I got you blood. I'm gonna have Roses call a bail bondsman and fix it. Just pull up on me once you get released." Red hung up and looked over at Bandz, shaking his head back and forth in disbelief. This would be the third time Red bailed out GoGetta within the past year.

GoGetta knew how to get a dollar. His only problem was that he spent it as soon as it came. His two major addictions - tricking on women and gambling - kept the money flowing. Red had grown up with him and they had been through a lot together.

CHAPTER 3

Red was posted up in front of Crackhead Henry's crib mingling with a few of his little homies. The crisp, fall air was refreshing and the block was real busy. It was the first of the month, which meant the local fiends were running around trying to get their fix.

All of a sudden, Red heard a voice cry out. "Bitch, I told your ass leave me alone about that already!" He looked up and saw Smoke screaming at his girl, then follow up his words with a backhand across her face.

The impact from the slap made her collapse between two parked cars. The block was packed, and quite a few people stopped to watch. Unfortunately, it had also gotten Red's attention.

"Yo leave Shorty alone Smoke," Red said. "Take that shit in the crib.

You making the block hot homie!" He stepped down from the stoop and approached the drama. As he got closer, Smoke started to back away.

Red had an established reputation around the neighborhood. He made sure everyone was good and tried to keep the community safe. He would rather have him and his homies patrol and protect the neighborhood than the corrupt N.Y.P.D. Ever since Razor left him in charge, his street cred kept going up.

Red approached the woman who was on the ground and reached out a hand to help her up. She was in her mid-50's and looked just like Angela Bassett on a good day.

"You punk ass nigga!" she shouted. "You lucky my son is in prison because he would have killed your ass." She took Red's hand, got up, and wiped the blood from her nose with a tissue.

A part of Smoke felt badly, so he came back and tried to help the lady walk home.

The woman immediately shook off his help. "Get off me right now!"

Red pushed Smoke back to try and avoid more drama before the police showed up. The block was a gold mine and the lil homies were trying to get money.

"Red this ain't got nothing to do with you youngsta." Smoke suddenly threw a haymaker that almost connected with Red's jaw. He missed, spun around, and then fell on the concrete face-first.

Red smelled liquor on Smoke's breath, but that wasn't enough to give him a pass on an ass-whooping. As Smoke tried to get up, Red's Timberland boot came crashing down on his left eye socket. Seven other bloods immediately came running across the street to assist their big homie. Even though he didn't need the help, they all had something to prove and were trying to earn some rank under the set.

Smoke was getting destroyed under pairs of knuckles and feet. In the midst of it, two patty wagons rolled up on the scene. A few onlookers screamed, "Po-Po!" but everyone was too caught up in the moment to notice.

"Everybody freeze!" an officer screamed. "Get down on the ground!' He had his right hand on his holster - something a lot of white officers did when they came to the hood.

The police were always trigger happy and thirsty to send up a parade of bullets. Two of Red's lil homies took off running like they were in a marathon. A few more officers jumped out and surrounded the rest of the gang.

Red thought about running until he felt a 9-millimeter pressed up against the back of his skull. "Don't make any sudden moves or I'll have to shoot you," the black officer said.

By this point, Smoke was on the floor, lying in the fetal position and holding the side of his ribs tightly. There was a lot of blood coming out of the side of his head as well.

"Now everybody get on your knees and lock your fingers behind your head." A chubby officer walked over and removed a set of handcuffs from his belt.

The first thing that Red could think of was just 'jail.' He didn't mind it, though. It was for a good cause. After watching his dad beat on his mom, he never liked to see men beating on women.

This would be his first time having a run-in with the law since his stint in juvie. He'd rather get detained for this than something really major.

Red was shackled on a bus with a bunch of gangstas, drug dealers, pimps, and whoever else was headed with him to Riker's Island. This was the city jail for people in all five boroughs. This was the spot that held the city's most notorious criminals. Even though New York had the Boat, the Tombs, and Brooklyn house, this was the wildest out of them all.

As Red stared out the window looking at East Elmhurst, he couldn't get over the fact that out of everyone in court, the judge only remanded him. That, along with all of the stories he had heard from the old heads, put him in gladiator mode. He just had to deal with the struggles until his next court appearance in a month.

As the bus crossed the long bridge to the island, Red saw enough buildings and barbed wire to secure twenty prisons. The bus stopped at C-74, dropped off a few people, then continued to the Beacon. That would be Red's home for the next month.

* * *

Red got finger-printed, had his photo taken for an I.D., and got stripped out. Wearing his new clothes, he stepped into a packed holding cell with a bunch of unfamiliar faces. After an hour of observing the 17 people in there with him, he heard an announcement.

"Jones, Medina, Anderson, Hawkins, and Scott. Come with me." A slim Hispanic lady with short brown hair motioned for the five inmates to follow her down the corridor. She pointed to a white bin with R&D printed on it. "Y'all go ahead and take a bed roll with you."

Continuing down the hall, the lady stopped in front of a metal detector. "After I give you these index cards you just walk past the metal detectors. Your housing units will be written on there so y'all will know where you're going." Red took his card and began to walk towards his unit.

As Red walked down the hallway he heard an alarm going off. He looked behind him and saw a bunch of officers running with helmets, shields, and batons. They were shouting and running towards 6 South, the same unit that Red was going to.

The Captain calmly walked down the hallway behind the officers. "Everyone face the wall and don't take your face from there unless told otherwise." There were only about 11 people scattered throughout the corridor, but they all turned to face the wall, including Red.

The inmates faced the wall for a good 20 minutes before the officers brought a light-skinned, freckled man out of 6 South. Red stole a quick glance to see them escort the shirtless man down the hallway. The whole experience was new for him and he wanted to be aware of his surroundings. Shortly after they escorted a second man down the hall. This one had blood gushing from his right cheek and splattered all over his white t-shirt.

A couple of minutes later, the captain returned to the hallway and let everyone know they could resume regular movement. "Hurry up and get to where you're going."

Red glanced at his index card and took a deep breath. He didn't know what awaited him on the other side of the door.

"Let me see that card in your hand." While Red waited at the door, an officer had opened it and now stood before him. He was dark-skinned, bald, and his voice dripped with authority. The officer glanced down at the photo on Red's index card, back up at Red, and then nodded. "Aight, come in here. This is your unit. Take bed number 20."

The second Red stepped into the dorm all eyes were drawn on him. It was like one of those movies where everyone stops what they are doing right in the middle. Not a single person was left not checking out the new guy.

"Yo what up blood - you bangin homie?" A stocky, caramel-complexioned man walked up to Red as he tied his black du-rag around his crispy waves.

"You already know b's up all day. This is Neighborhood Gangstas over here!" Red threw up the B with his right hand and kept his voice serious.

Another dark-skinned fat dude approached. "Put your bedroll on your bunk and come in the T.V. room to meet the rest of the damus."

Red did as he was told. As he got to the T.V. room, there were about eight faces staring back at him. Each was unfamiliar, and each looked menacing.

A tall, slim, brown-skinned dude with cornrows stepped up to Red. He went to throw up the universal Blood handshake, but instead two-pieced Red in the face. One shot hit him in the left eye, and the other in the jaw.

"C'z up nigga, this is a Crip house homie!"

Once the brown-skinned cat said that, the rest of the men rushed Red in a flurry of punches and kicks dealt all over his body.

Red had been accustomed to the gang life since he was little. He already knew all he could do was embrace the war and represent his set to the fullest. He had always had a finely sculpted body, but as he grew older his muscle mass had him looking like a baby Tookie Williams. His muscles Were bulging everywhere.

As Red rumbled with eight people, he managed to stay on top of all of them. Not only did he not fall over, he quickly knocked out three of the assailants.

After seeing three guys fall over, the Crips began to throw chairs at Red. The noise level escalated as Red had his back against the wall, swinging and bobbing for his life. He was just hoping that none of them swung a blade to cut open his face.

Suddenly the C.O. burst into the room. "Aight, aight. Leave the new dude alone." The violence stopped immediately, and the officer walked over to Red. "Medina, you want to move to another unit?" He looked over the new guy and was concerned for his well-being.

Red laughed. "Nah, I'm good where I'm at." He never felt comfortable being off-point or falling asleep. He was alright with being in a unit with crips as long as he did it on his own terms.

As soon as he got back to his bed, Red put two bars of soap out of his hygiene pack into a large, white sock. Then he tied a knot at the bottom to secure the soap. He got off his bunk once the lights went out and silently crept towards the bathroom.

Besides a few people snoring, the dorm was dead quiet. When Red got to the bathroom, he looked in the mirror and noticed a nice-sized lump over his right eye. The sight of that enraged him even more. Red's complexion was high yellow, and any mark, scratch, or lump showed.

Red grumbled as he left the bathroom. Taking a left, he noticed one of the crip dudes from the T.V. room lying in bed, fast asleep.

Red ran over to the bed and started swinging the soap-in-a-sock at him, instantly cracking open his head.

After the fourth swing, the crip realized what was happening to him.

"Ahhh - what the fuck homie chill out!" He jumped out of bed and began to run around the dorm. "Help me cuz! Help me cuz!"

Red chased him with the sock, continuing the assault even after the C.O. cut on the lights.

What everyone saw once the lights came on looked like a scene straight out of "The Hills Have Eyes." There was blood everywhere. Red had broken the dude's nose and split his head open to the bone. By now, the majority of the dorm had woken up and witnessed the last part of the fight.

Red looked around at the dorm with a menacing grin, and pounded on his chest like a silverback gorilla. "y'all niggas thought it was sweet? B's up!"

Everyone went silent as the female C.O. walked over to assess the situation. She saw all the blood first, then looked around for the perpetrator of this incident. "Holy shit! Is that you? Nelson Medina?"

Red did a double-take. It was his cousin, Cathy. They hadn't seen each other since Red went in for his first bid in juvie. She used to work in Spofford Juvenile Facility, where he was initially placed before going up to Brookwood in upstate NY.

"Alright everybody, go back to sleep. Ain't nothing to be nosy about." She turned to Red. "Nelson, come to the bubble once I cut the lights off." Cathy walked off back towards her office as most of the crips went to the bathroom to huddle up.

* * *

Throughout the next couple weeks, Red fought every single day for respect in the unit. He found out that he was the only one claiming blood in the entire dorm. The other crips ended up beating up the dude Red had messed up at night, and ran him out of the unit. They felt as though he was a coward for screaming like he did. Thankfully Red didn't even have to go to the box for solitary confinement for the fight Cathy hadn't hit her body alarm.

Red found out that Cathy had told Soulchild, the head crip, to stitch the dude up with some thread and put ice on his nose.

Today had been a day like any other, and by early afternoon Red was writing a letter on his bed, until he heard the C.O. yell out. "Medina, Santiago, Powell, Rivera, Mitchell. Y'all got visits."

Red had been here for two weeks with only phone calls and letters, so a visit was very unexpected. He instantly sprang up from the bed and started to get ready.

After waiting at the door for all the inmates to arrive, the 7 walked down together to the visiting room. Red changed into a visit grey jumper and slippers, then peeked into the room to see who had come to visit him.

Scanning the room of faces, he saw the Bloodette Roses sitting by herself dressed in all red. The second the C.O. opened the door, she jumped out of her seat and started waving at Red.

"Yo blood - over here!" Roses smiled as Red walked up, and greeted him with the neighborhood handshake. Then she pulled Red close and grabbed his crotch while tongue-kissing him passionately.

In the midst of the kiss, Red felt her spit two balloons the size of jawbreakers into his mouth. He tasted the rubber and swallowed both balloons instantly. Eventually, they broke off their kiss and sat down next to each other.

"Blood, those are from GoGetta. Him and Bandz drove me here to come see you."

"I should have known your ass was coming through." He smiled at Roses and caressed her leg.

"They both send their love and respect. Bandz also talked with your lawyer. He said you're gonna beat this gang assault charge cause Smoke refuses to testify. In fact, some of the little homies ran him out of the hood." Roses smiled and knew that Red would be back home soon.

Before the two could continue their conversation, they both heard someone yelling Red's name from another part of the visiting room.

Red turned around and saw the woman that Smoke had slapped from the hood. She was sitting next to Soulchild in a visit. Red waved at her, caught eye contact with Soulchild, then turned back to Roses to continue their conversation.

Time flew, and soon everyone was saying their last goodbyes. All over the visiting room, dudes were getting their last kisses, hugs, and feels on. Red was still stuck on why that lady came to see the crip nigga.

Red threw up the neighborhood handshake with

Roses, then made his way to the back to get strip searched. As he waited, Soulchild walked up and tapped him on the shoulder.

"Ayo Red, my mom Dukes told me what happened with you and Smoke. I appreciate that - real talk. From here on out, you good in 6 South." Soulchild held out his right hand to shake with Red.

"No doubt Loc, but got to keep it 120% with you. I'm gonna be good regardless of where I'm at and who's around." Red gripped Souldhild hand to return the shake and show respect. He appreciated the gesture, but also held firm in any situation he was a part of.

In the following week, Red and Soulchild grew real tight. They both realized they had many similarities, shared the same values, and had so much in common. They both grew up without a father and quickly rose to the top of their respective neighborhood gangs. The only real difference was that one is a Crip and the other a blood.

The two exchanged information and made plans for when both were back in society. Red knew that he was going home soon. Not only did he have one of the best attorneys' out of the Bronx, the D.A. couldn't even locate Smoke to testify. Soulchild, on the other hand, was just waiting on a trial date. He was convinced he could beat the murder charge he was facing.

Soulchild was originally from Flatbush, Brooklyn out of the 90's, but his mother left for the Bronx after he caught the body. She didn't want to be around for the aftermath of her son's actions. Everyone knows in the streets that every action has a reaction. Soulchild caught the man down on a robbery that went sour. What he didn't know was the guy he killed was a very important member of the infamous Shower Posse...

CHAPTER 4

Red tongued down Indiana passionately while his two hands roamed around her exquisite body. At one point, he got so into the kissing session that he almost fell off the edge of her queen-size bed. Just when he thought he had the upper hand, in one swift motion Indiana managed to climb on top of Red. Their lips were glued together and tongues were wrestling for control. The love between the two had always been electrifying.

Red's mind was completely controlled by liquor and lust. He gave in and started to pull down Indiana's pajama pants, revealing her voluptuous backside. He felt around and realized she wasn't wearing any panties. That gave him an instant hard-on. He sucked on her neck and pressed his growing erection against her thigh.

Indiana felt Red's hard erection and her pussy

juices started flowing like a waterfall. Immediately, she began to unbuckle Red's Fendi belt and pop the buttons on his jeans. As she took care of his pants, she felt Red's middle and index fingers enter her warm, wet vagina.

Just when she thought she couldn't get any more turned on, Red went and satisfied her cravings even more. Indiana began to slowly grind on his two fingers in a circular motion, and then rode his fingers like a cowgirl. She arched her back and threw her head back, enjoying the immense pleasure.

Red licked his lips, watching his girl ride his fingers, and couldn't take it anymore. "Baby, get in doggystyle position for me." He removed his fingers and watched Indiana get down on all fours. Just the sight of her bent over displaying her meaty pussy lips - completely shaven - got him going. With his pulsating rod in his right hand, Red bit his bottom lip and prepared to enter her.

Red crawled over on the bed, held Indiana with his left hand, and shoved his dick aggressively in her pussy. He put both hands on her love handles and started long-stroking her at a steady pace.

"Ahh! Ohh! Damn, Red! Destroy this pussy, daddy!"

Indiana gripped the bed sheets tightly as she got the pounding of her life. She started throwing her ass back at Red, looking back at him and biting her bottom lip seductively at him.

Red had been staring down, watching his manhood slide in and out of her love tunnel. When she started really getting into it, he picked up his pace and started thrusting in faster and faster. Pretty soon, the only sounds in the bedroom were Red's balls smacking against Indiana's clit over and over, and her moaning.

"Go faster, daddy! I'm about to cum!" She screamed louder and louder as Red's throbbing cock went faster and faster into her dripping pussy. "Oh my god - please don't stop! Uhh - uhh - uhh - ohhh, Ohhh!!"

The sensation from her tight walls had Red in pure ecstasy. He wanted to nut inside her so badly, but managed to hold off. After she came all over his manhood he stroked her a few more times, then pulled out. "Ayo ma - put this in your mouth."

Red wiggled it in her face as he stood up at the edge of the bed.

Indiana sat up indian-style on the bed and put Red's dick in her mouth faster than a homeless person scarfing down food at an all-you-can-eat buffet. Her head bobbed up and down frantically as saliva dripped everywhere. It felt so good that Red closed his eyes and wrapped Indiana's long, jet-black hair around his fist.

Between her gagging noises and the way her tongue ring rubbed against him, Red couldn't hold in his nut any longer. Indiana must have known he was about to cum because she started to speed up her sucking even more. As he felt the nut, she kept going until she had swallowed every last drop of semen he had. Red was lucky to have a girl like Indiana who was so crazy in love with him.

Indiana continued to spit, lick, and suck until Red's manhood came back to full attention. "Are you ready for round two?" She unsnapped her bra, exposing a set of perky 36 D's and bit her soft, pink bottom lip.

Red shook his head up and down, anticipating the session that was about to take place. "Lay down on your back. It's my turn to have your toes curling." Red bent down and parted her thighs...

At least three times every week, the lovers made time for their late-night rendezvous. No matter what, when one called the other they would both drop what they were doing to meet up. Their physical attraction to each other was undeniable, but their soul connection was magnetic. There was something about Indiana that made Red put his guard down. If there was anyone in the world that knew Red, it was her. There was definitely a future for the two of them together.

Indiana wasn't no hood rat; she was about something in life and her mentality was beyond the average woman. Indiana was currently enrolled in the police academy. If there's one thing for sure about love, it's that your heart falls for the one it wants to.

* * *

In May 2015, fate and opportunity intertwined and made it possible for Red and Indiana to cross paths. Red was cruising around in a forest-green 3 Series with the top down, enjoying City Island in the Bronx. While he scanned the sidewalks, he spotted Indiana standing in front of Ohana's 3 Restaurant alone.

She stood about 5'5" with jet-black long hair, a mocha complexion, big brown eyes, nice firm breasts, big pink full lips, and a nice round ass. Red saw her and did a double-take. He immediately busted a u-turn to try his hand. Red pulled up his car next to her and licked his lips. "Excuse me sweetheart - can I steal a few minutes of your time?" As he spoke, his eyes roamed up and down her beautiful body.

"So that's how you speak to women? Yelling at them from a distance?" Indiana looked him over and folded her arms across her chest. "At least have the courtesy to get out of your car and approach me."

Red hit his blinkers, double-parked his car, and got out. As he got closer to her, she could smell his cologne.

"Hi - my name is Nelson but everybody calls me

Red. You are very elegant ma. And I figured if I ain't approach you now I might have let you slip away." Red put out his right hand to shake hers.

She smiled at him and ignored the proffered hand, giving him a hug instead. "My name is Indiana. Nice to meet you. But can I ask, what is the name of that cologne? I love that smell."

"Why would I tell you that? So you can have the next nigga wearing that around you?" Red lifted his right eyebrow a bit.

Indiana saw this and laughed.

"So who you out here with - your boyfriend?" Red stared deep into her eyes.

"My homegirl Mindy and my godbrother Walter."

Red glanced down at his phone and realized that he was running late. "I don't mean to cut this short but can I have your number so we can stay in contact? I'm running late to my homie's studio session."

The two exchanged numbers and said their farewells. Even after leaving, Red couldn't erase the image of Indiana's fine ass out of his head. The combination-of her character and beauty had him mesmerized.

While he was at the session at the studio, he still couldn't get her out of his head. He decided to call her. He didn't want to seem thirsty but couldn't help it. She picked up on the second ring. "Yo Indiana I know we just left, but I wanna see you again if it's possible."

"The funny thing is that I was just debating on calling you. I just dropped off my people; - where you at? Text me an address and I'll meet you there."

Indiana pulled up to the studio and Red walked up to her silver Nissan Sentra, noting the police sticker on the windshield. He got in the car and sat there talking with her for hours until the sun rose. It was definitely love at first sight.

Neither wanted to leave the other's company. They talked about everything: goals, past relationships, likes and dislikes. By the end of their conversation it was like they had known each other all their lives.

From that day forward, the two were inseparable. That would be the first day of many they would spend together.

* * *

Alex Kujovich was the son of the notorious Russian mobster Michael Kujovich, AKA Mikey Fingaz. Mikey, a boss in the Russian mob, was born in Moscow, moved to Los Angeles at the age of five, and raised there in California by his mother. He rose up through the ranks in L.A. until he got a top dog for the Florencia 13 killed over drug turf.

Around the same time, Mikey Fingaz found out his wife was pregnant with his son Alex. He relocated his family to Miami to avoid the retaliation for the murder. What he didn't know was that the Florencia 13 had ties to a higher power. They had a hitman locate Mikey in Florida and put the green light on him.

Fortunately for him, the hit ended up messy and Mikey was able to slip away. He moved one more time, along with his wife and newborn son, to Williamsburg, Brooklyn. He had some family and comrades living close and knew they would be well protected.

It took him almost no time to invest into real estate, the drug trade, and solidify a foundation for his family. He opened up two strip clubs, a gambling spot, and a restaurant within three years. Mikey Fingaz eventually guided his son Alex and taught him how to keep his operations running once he was old enough. Over time, Alex began generating lucrative revenue just like his dad, and only had to reach out if there was an issue out of his control. That rarely happened..until recently.

Alex got a call from his mom, telling him that his uncle had been murdered. She was upset - it was her brother! Mikey Fingaz was enraged and put his ear to the streets to find out who had murdered his brother-in-law.

To get results faster, Mikey offered a $10,000 reward to anyone who provided accurate information.

* * *

Ever since Red became a free man, he and Soulchild had maintained a strong relationship. Red kept his promise to his friend and held him down in jail. Soulchild was still waiting for a trial date since the D.A. kept asking for extensions. Their case was weak: there was no gun and no witnesses willing to testify. Everything was based off here say and the fact that his name kept coming up.

You know how the streets talk: some things be speculation and others factual.

Aside from his normal day-to-day activities and holding Soulchild down, Red had been spending even more time with Indiana. The two were even considering moving in together. In such a short period of time things had escalated quickly between the two.

Before Red started dealing with Indiana, he never really took any woman seriously. For most of his life, money was the main focus. Occasionally, he would slide off and entertain a few different women.

Most women in the neighborhood wouldn't even try to get at Red because they knew Roses would go insane. She had had a few incidents already with other women who came around. A few got beaten up, while two others now had scars on their faces.

Red and Roses had never had a real relationship, just sex sessions. Even though they were just fuck buddies, she was protective of him.

Red couldn't envision himself settling down with a woman living the same lifestyle as he was. He really wanted to settle down, become legit, and have children eventually. For now, he was the weed man. He had the best prices for pounds and dealt with the Neighborhood Gangstas out in California, receiving it through the mail.

Because Red was so caught up with getting money, he never really paid attention to Roses' feelings. Her motto became, if she couldn't have Red then nobody could have him.

Nobody in the hood ever got to fuck Roses but Red. Everybody was under the impression they were serious. Red was the one who took Roses' virginity, so she was sprung in love with Red.

Roses was beautiful and you would never think she was a gang member. She stood at 5'9", had a caramel complexion, brown eyes, diamond-stud nose ring, rocked the Hallie Berry short cut, and had a body that Mr. Miami couldn't construct.

CHAPTER 5

Three months later...

It was a beautiful sunny day and everyone in the hood was outside enjoying the weather. There wasn't a single cloud in the sky, birds were singing, and kids were playing in the streets.

"Hey Roses, look at your man pulling up right now." Apple pointed to the car as she put lip gloss on her lips. She was with a group of bloodettes standing in front of Roses' building. They were about ten deep.

Red pulled up in front of the crowd. He was there to serve the homie GoGetta a few pounds before taking Indiana out to eat at Pine's Restaurant. Indiana was sitting in the passenger seat texting on her phone as Red got out of the car.

As soon as he stepped out, everybody flocked to him and started saluting. Indiana got curious and came out of the car as well. As she approached the scene, everybody stared at her.

Roses' stare was the most menacing, and her mind was flooded with embarrassment and rage. "Yo blood - who this bitch right here?" Her-face was twisted up in a grimace.

Red smiled and turned to the crowd. "Everybody, I want to introduce y'all to my wifey Indiana."

Roses' heart dropped into her stomach. She always assumed she was going to be the one Red would settle down with. He had never presented a woman as his wifey before. She had grown up with Red and known him all her life. Right now, she definitely felt a certain way.

Red turned to his wifey. "Indiana, get back in the car. Let me give this to my homie in the building and we out after that." He planted a passionate kiss on her lips and walked into the building.

As Indiana walked back towards the car, she heard a nasty voice behind her.

"Yo bitch, what's good?" Roses walked towards Indiana, taking out her earrings. "When you started fucking with my man?"

Indiana tied her hair up in a bun. "Look shorty, you got me all the way messed up." She already knew where this interaction was headed.

When Roses got close enough Indiana threw a vicious right hook that connected with Roses' cheek. She quickly followed up with a left jab that busted up her lip. The rest of the bloodettes watched from a distance, not trying to disrespect Red's wifey. Roses was on her own in this situation.

Red walked out of the building and saw a crowd gathered around two individuals on the sidewalk. He pushed people out of the way to see what was happening.

When he got to the center of the circle, he saw Roses sprawled up in the fetal position while Indiana was stomping her out.

Red ran at the two women. "Y'all bugging out! Get off of her Indiana, chill out!"

The sound of Red's voice put an end to the ass-whooping Indiana was giving Roses. Red took Indiana by the hand and escorted her back to the car. Once inside, he went back over to see what was up with Roses. He knew that she had started this whole ordeal, and was actually shocked Roses was the one who got beat up.

"You okay ma?" Red held out a hand to help her up off the sidewalk.

"Nigga don't touch me!" Roses screamed, batting away his hand. "Go ahead and get the fuck out of here. I hate you Red!" Tears streamed down her cheeks; and blood stained her face. Not only was her lip busted, blood dripped from out both of her nostrils as well.

"Aight then, have it your way. I'm out of here." Red turned and walked towards his car. "Yo Apple

- help your friend out blood." He jumped into his smoke-grey 535i BMW.

Red turned to his right and saw Indiana's chest heaving. She had her head leaned back in the headrest and her eyes were closed.

"Damn Red, I can't believe you got me into this situation. I ain't know you were like a Blood Messiah out here. I didn't even know you were in a gang." Indiana slowly shook her head from side to side.

"First off, I ain't get you into shit. Secondly I thought you put two and two together by all the red I be rocking. I was raised in this gang life. I just get money - I ain't with the ignorant shit no more."

On the drive to the restaurant, Indiana actually found herself turned on by the street power she saw that Red possessed. They might have been from two completely different worlds, but opposites definitely attract.

* * *

Not only did Red and Roses go to all the same schools growing up, they were raised in the same neighborhood. Roses' grandmother Porsha and Red's mother Jennifer worked together at the Hunt's Point Terminal Market. Since they were cool, Red and Roses were around each other all the time.

At first they played hood games like hide and

seek, truth or dare, and spin the bottle. As the two got older and their hormones started taking over, curiosity started to intervene. It started off with simple kisses, then grew to include tongues. As the years progressed, Roses' body started developing and Red began finger-popping her because she wasn't ready just yet.

The two were inseparable from each other. When Red began to be hypnotized by the gang world, their time with each other grew less and less. Red became addicted to the alluring streets until one slip-up cost him a stint in juvie.

Roses was devastated when she heard Red had been locked up, but rode out the whole three years with him. She went on visits with his mom, wrote Red letters every week, and sent him pictures. When he got home from Brookwood, she finally let him take her virginity. That only made her fall deeper in love with him - even joining the bloods.

Roses used her beauty to benefit the set. She used to bait ballers and get them robbed by Razor, Red, and Krazy. Roses was a loyal female, blinded by love and loyalty. As time progressed she started gaining rank within the Neighborhood Gangstas.

Because of their long history, Roses was hurt to find out Red had crowned another woman his queen. Red was the only man she had ever known. In her eyes, Red was the one she needed - the only one.

CHAPTER 6

Red, Bandz, and GoGetta skipped the long line of people and went straight to the entrance to Show Palace, a strip club down the block from the Queensbridge projects. As they arrived at the front of the line, one of the bouncers recognized Red instantly.

"Yo big bro! What's good with you? What that neighborhood like?" The big, bald-headed bouncer walked towards him.

"What the fuck is good with you Flex!" Red's excitement dripped through his voice. The two threw up the neighborhood handshake and embraced. "How much we gotta give you to slide up in here with the grip?"

Flex looked him in the eyes. "Give me the hammer and I'll give it back once you're inside. I got you." Flex held out his right hand for the gun.

Red passed it off and started walking towards the metal detectors. The three went through, were searched, and stepped inside the club.

As the room opened up, Red saw naked women packed in everywhere. All types of exotic beauties kept walking past. This strip club was fully nude. They didn't sell any liquor - only beer and hookah.

Red looked around and finally his eyes settled on a cinnamon-colored woman with shirley temples in her hair sliding down a pole upside-down. His eyes were glued to her goddess body for a few minutes until he was interrupted by a tap on his shoulders.

"Yo bro," Flex said. "Come follow me to the bathroom so I can give you this grip."

Red followed Flex to the bathroom and took the chrome 25 from him with a smile.

Flex frowned. "Blood you really don't need that up in here. It's about ten of my little homies in here over in V.I.P. Come on - let me introduce you to them while I'm roaming. Because they gonna call me back to my post soon."

The two left the bathroom and began walking through the packed crowd. As they walked through, there was a blond, blue-eyed dancer staring at Red. Her face seemed so familiar, but he couldn't seem to remember where he had seen her.

"Ayo Bro, I see you staring at her right there. Her name is Amber and you should go in the private

rooms with her. She will definitely entertain you."
Flex pointed at Amber dancing on stage.

As the D.J. blended in a new song, Red heard
someone shout. "Ayo Skrap, we over here with the
homies!" Red looked over and saw Bandz with his
hands in the air waving wildly.

Amber noticed Red and thought the same thing
- she had definitely seen this man before. Then her
attention diverted to the man waving in the air.
There was something about Bandz' voice that
sounded familiar. Suddenly it hit her. She heard
the words, "Come on Skrap, let's go. We been here
way too long." She would never forget those words,
nor the same raspy voice that Bandz had that said
them. The night when her father was murdered in
front of her haunted her until this day. Amber
looked closer at Bandz and saw that he had the
same build as one of the men that had robbed that
gambling spot in the Bronx.

Bandz' 300-pound frame was unique in the club.
He used it to move the crowd aside to let Flex and
Red in the V.I.P. area. Flex introduced Red to
everybody before going back to work. Usually, Red
kept his circle smaller than a decimal, so he only
dealt with a handful of homies.

Red looked around and saw everyone smoking
hookah and drinking beers. Red didn't do either, so
he started to roll up a blunt on one of the couches.
He bobbed his head to Young Ma's song "Oouuhh"

and looked up when the D.J. shouted out the name Blueprint.

There was another V.I.P. section across from Red where he saw a light-skinned cat with long cornrows and a blue bandanna throw up a "C" at the D.J. He turned to one of the young homies who confirmed that was Blueprint. As Red looked closer, he noticed everyone in the other section was wearing blue clothing.

Red leaned over and lit his blunt just as a short Dominican dancer started shaking her thick behind in Red's face. The yellow g-string she wore was swallowed completely by her ass cheeks. She was not only elegant, but topless as well. The Spanish mami was putting on a show for him, but Red's eyes wandered until he saw Bandz with a white stripper. It was rare to see a white woman built like shorty was. She looked like Ice-T's wife CoCo in so many ways.

Bandz' right hand palmed her ass cheek as they sipped beers by the bar. His phone buzzed, and as he checked it Amber slipped a small pill into his beer.

"Hey I wanna take you to the back rooms and give you a private show." Amber grabbed Bandz' dick through his jeans and winked seductively.

"Right come on then I definitely need that." Bandz started to follow her to the back. "You think you gonna be able to handle a nigga like me?"

Bandz followed her through the crowd, eventually coming to the back area where there were eight rooms. Each room had gold curtains with purple ropes and was guarded by one of three white bouncers. She led Bandz to the last room, sat him down on the black velvet couch, and started dancing on him.

After a few minutes, Bandz started to feel woozy and passed out. Amber immediately went through his pockets, pulling out a wad of cash, pack of cigarettes, and a Galaxy phone.

Amber and a few of the other dancers practiced this exact routine every week on numerous men. The Show Palace was a corrupt Gentleman's club. Aside from scamming men, they also sold drugs and ran a prostitution ring.

When Amber had everything she wanted, she abandoned the scene and went upstairs to the owner's office. Amber knocked three times on the door, then entered and walked up to the desk.

"Here you go." Amber dropped the money and phone on the desk and stepped back from the owner.

Alex looked down at the money, then back up at Amber. "I told you last week - we can't rob people and pull tricks no more! We getting too much heat on us and the police got a whiff of everything going on here." He stood up and back-handed Amber right on the eye. "Next time listen and don't let this happen again."

Just as Alex was about to continue his speech, he heard three shots fired. He ran to the window, which gave him an overview of the entire club. All he could see from here was people running around frantically. The lights were dim but he could see the crowd all shifting towards the exit, while the bouncers ran towards the commotion.

Red knew exactly what he was doing. His specialty was hitting his target on sight and getting away with it. He had crept through the crowd with his chrome 25 and found his target. Red grabbed Blueprint's neck, pulling it close and whispering in his ear. "This is from Soulchild nigga!"

- BLAM - BLAM - BLAM -

Red let off three bullets in Blueprint's skull and his limp body collapsed instantly. There were traces of blood and brain matter splattered all over Red's skully and face.

The club was still in chaos, but the bouncers tried to control the situation before police arrived.

Red walked by Flex, leaning in close. "Yo blood make sure you get the security video."

"Don't worry homie they haven't been working the past few days. You good!"

Red wiped off his face and slid quickly back to his car. Because this club was very strict on security, this was the only opportunity Red had to pull this off. The likelihood Blueprint would be armed inside was slim to none.

Red had planned and mapped out the night in excruciating detail. Those who fail to plan plan to fail. Red always planned to succeed and would always stand on his word.

Jasmin was fuming mad. The night before, Blueprint had put his hands
on her after getting drunk. Even if she was his baby momma, she wasn't about to take that shit from any man. That's why she went to go visit her brother Soulchild at Riker's Island.

"Yo bro real shit - my baby father been really feeling himself lately! He been talking mad shit about you and how Neighborhood Rollin 60's is his now." She looked up at her brother with anger in her eyes. "He been power- drunk lately and even put his hands on me."

Soulchild sat in front of his sister in the visiting room, jaw clenched and eyes wide at her words. Unfortunately, his sister wasn't the first person to tell him any of this. Most of his anger was at Blueprint, but some was at himself for ignoring the problem too long.

Soulchild and Blueprint were real tight before he got locked up. He was Soulchild's right-hand man - which is why hearing these facts again hurt him so much.

"Oh yea sis? He talking crazy like that?" Tears started to form among the fire in his eyes. "Look - I can't let the set go into shambles behind one person. So I gotta get him hit - it's only right."

"Look don't worry about my nephew Stephen," Soulchild continued. "I got him and he'll be well taken care of."

Jasmin continued to stare at her brother. She understood where he was coming from. Her loyalty has always been to her family and she wasn't about to change now. "Okay then. How is this all going down? So I can get everything out him now?" She started to grin. Jasmin had never been in love with Blueprint. He was really just there for the drunk sex, and she had accidentally gotten pregnant.

"I'm gonna give you a phone number when I call later. Call that number and tell the guy I said that I wanna cash out on my favor now."

Soulchild got back to his unit and called up Jasmin, giving her Red's number to call. He didn't want the Crips to know he was behind the hit. Plus, Red was already familiar with the situation. He had seen photos of Blueprint when he was locked up with Soulchild.

Jasmin ended up giving red the drop on Blueprint the night of the murder.

Everyone had crossed their T's and dotted their I's. Every move gotta have purpose and direction.

CHAPTER 7

"I think it's time to take down the Kujovich Dynasty. Tonight." Detective Griffin slammed his hand down on his desk, rattling the coffee cups that rested there.

Sergeant Burgos slowly considered a jelly donut. "Let's not get ahead of ourselves buddy. The only person we actually have evidence on is Alex Kujovich. The rest of the empire is clean."

Griffin put down a coffee and wiped powdered sugar from his bulbous beard. "One of my informants showed me proof that their strip club, Show Palace, is full of corruption. They sell drugs, run a prostitution ring, and make this precinct look like shit!"

Burgos took a big bite out of the donut. "Let me see the proof you got that all those things are going on at the establishment."

Detective Griffin pulled out his phone and flipped through a few videos his informant had sent him. He watched the Sergeant as his jaw began to drop.

"Send this to my phone. There's plenty of crime taking place there. It's time to show this to the captain."

* * *

One month later...

After the Captain saw the footage, he immediately reached out to a judge to get a warrant issued and signed for Alex Kujovich. They planned the hit at 3 am when the club was mostly empty.

Unmarked cars surrounded the Show Palace. All of the dancers were still inside, along with a few stragglers. Alex was in his office, sniffing lines of cocaine with one of the strippers. He had just had an argument with his father on the phone.

Mikey Fingaz was getting sick and tired of his son holding back information from him and doing whatever the fuck he wanted. He had told him so in no uncertain terms on the phone call.

"My dad is an arrogant motherfucker! It's either his way or the highway." Alex laughed and snorted another line, falling back into his plush, leather chair. The stripper's titties were at perfect eye level as he gazed forward. Just as he was about to say something, his office door came crashing down.

"Freeze asshole! It's N.Y.P.D. Put your hands up now!" An older, white officer with salt and pepper hair had his .45 trained straight at Alex.

He had been so high on cocaine he hadn't paid attention to any of the security cameras. How the hell had the police made it inside? And the Captain was on their payroll too - except Alex had forgotten to send him the payment last week.

While the officer slipped handcuffs on Alex, a female officer cuffed the stripper. Both of them were seated on top of the desk as the other ten officers ransacked the office. During the search, they found two unregistered handguns, 50 grams of cocaine, and $60,000 cash in the open safe. Things kept adding up for the indictment.

Officer Knight turned to the older male officer. "Hey Smith! Help me take the woman outside to the van parked out front."

Walking outside in cuffs, Alex saw people getting handcuffed left and right. Some were even attempting to cooperate instantly with the police before they even left the building.

* * *

"Where is Uncle Mikey at? I need to speak with him. Urgently." Amber paced back and forth as she waited in the kitchen with her aunt.

"He should be back any minute," Barbara replied. "He just called me before you got here." She continued to chop up the broccoli for their dinner that evening.

After about fifteen minutes, Mikey Fingaz came through the front door along with his under-boss Rolo. Amber could tell they were in the middle of a very angry conversation.

"...and how the hell could that happen?" Mikey yelled.

Amber pulled out a phone from her jacket pocket. "Uncle Mikey can I talk to you real quick? It's very important." She showed him the phone. "Look at this right here!"

The phone screen showed a photo of one of Mikey Fingaz' gambling spots in the Bronx.

"Okay, why you have a picture of this in your phone?" Mikey was puzzled and didn't know what Amber was getting at.

"This ain't my phone! It's a guy I took it from. Not only did he have this photo, the dumbass flaunted a bunch of money after the spot got robbed." She grabbed the phone back and scrolled through. "His phone wasn't even locked when I got it. His pics from Instagram and Facebook fit the description of the shooter who killed my dad." Tears started rolling down her cheeks.

Mikey grabbed the phone back. "Let me see his

pictures." He clenched his jaw and started to scroll. What stuck out to him was all the red bandanas in his photos. Back in California, blue meant Crips or Surenos and red meant Bloods or Nortenos. Since MS-13 was the only gang even close to Mexican in New York, that ruled out the Nortenos. Plus Bandz was dark-skinned, so he was probably a Blood.

Mikey kept scrolling and found a photo with the caption, "Blood gang or don't bang." There had been whispers on the streets, but this was the most accurate confirmation he had so far.

"Rolo I need you to dig up as much information on this fat motherfucker as possible. Get me everything from his favorite fast-food restaurant to his mother's address!" Mikey was still pissed, but now had somewhere specific to direct his anger.

* * *

"Damn baby - why you looking so stressed out? Come here and give me some love." Red spread his arms open wide and sat on the couch, waiting for Indiana to walk over to him. The two had recently moved into the same place together. They bought a house out in Bronxville and their relationship had blossomed into something both unique and real.

"Honey I'm tired, I ain't really that stressed out." Indiana dropped a manilla folder on the kitchen table and headed towards Red's arms. The two embraced and shared a brief, but passionate kiss.

Lately the two hadn't been in each other's presence consistently. Both of their schedules had been hectic. Red hustled in the streets and ran the set and Indiana had her police duties to take care of. Things between the two of them had been slightly distant lately.

Indiana kissed him one more time then stood up. "Let me jump in the shower so I can be relaxed. I want to enjoy some quality time with you." She began to peel off her clothes seductively as she walked down to the bathroom.

A few minutes went by, and curiosity got the better of Red. He walked over to the dining room table and opened up the manilla folder. Inside were some photos of different men, each labeled with their names. He started to leaf through the photos, but none of them looked familiar to him. What caught his attention was a piece of paper that said, "Kujovich Family." Red knew they were tied to the Russian Mafia.

The next page made Red sit down in the chair in surprise. He saw a photo of the gambling spot that he and Bandz had robbed. The next photo shocked him even more. Roses was wearing a red wig and thong dancing on a pole in the same spot. Red wasn't sure what to do next.

Just then Indiana called out from the bedroom.

"Baby come upstairs. I wanna cuddle up and watch some Netflix with you."

Red walked up the stairs and began to strategize. He needed to get Indiana to open up and discuss some of the details that were in that folder. He wanted to know just how much information they had and exactly what they knew.

CHAPTER 8

Three weeks later...

"Go around the block one more time. That was him from the photo!" Rolo put a full clip into his .40 cal and sat back in the passenger seat. It was 8 am and the neighborhood was a ghost town. There were a few fiends lingering and the dope dealers were out, but no one else to be seen.

As they spun around the block one more time, Rolo pointed at GoGetta. "That's definitely him. Pull up."

GoGetta was posted in front of a building by himself, drinking a Sunny Delight and scanning the block slowly. A black Benz S550 pulled up to the curb in front of him, all the windows tinted out. Immediately GoGetta knew something was up.

Rolo's man slid down the window and GoGetta

saw there were a bunch of Caucasian men inside. He reached for his waist and realized he had left his gun upstairs at Apple's apartment last night. Normally there are only two types of white people that come into the hood: police and drug addicts. Something didn't add up here.

"Yo man - me and my friends are trying to buy an 8 ball of some crack. Can you help us out?" Rolo yelled from the passenger seat. "We are from Jersey but got stuck out here last night at my cousin's party."

GoGetta stared at Rolo, trying to read his vibe and see if these were actual fiends or the feds. Because he knew the local police from having so many run-ins with the law, he knew they had to be big time.

"I ain't got nothing but the loudest of the loud, Playboy."

"How much you charge for an eighth?" Rolo leaned forward in the car.

"And what type of weed is it?"

"Give me $30 for the eighth and it's blueberry kush." GoGetta reached into his pocket and pulled out a ziploc bag filled with eighths bagged up and ready to go.

Rolo flashed a hundred-dollar bill at GoGetta, and he walked up to the car. As he got to the window, the driver pulled GoGetta's right arm through it. Simultaneously, two huge Russians tatted up got out of the car and rushed him. One began punching him in the ribs while the other put him in a headlock.

"Yo what the fuck are y'all doing to my man?" Apple screamed from the second floor apartment window. "Leave him alone!"

Rolo got out of the car, ran to the back, and popped the trunk open. GoGetta tried to fight back, but his 150-pound frame stood no chance against the Russian onslaught. They threw him in the trunk and sped off before anyone else saw what was happening.

Rolo and his boys drove back to Brooklyn to an abandoned house on Scholes Street in Williamsburg. The entire time, GoGetta was kicking at the trunk and yelling at the top of his lungs. It seemed like forever just to get to Brooklyn from the Bronx.

Suddenly the car stopped and the trunk popped open. GoGetta saw Rolo with his gun trained at his face.

"Look," Rolo started. "My boss just wants to speak with you briefly and we're gonna drop you back off on your block."

Each huge Russian reached to grab-GoGetta with the two biggest holding an arm since they didn't have time to tie him up. No one wanted him to run.

They dragged GoGetta to an abandoned house,

and Rolo smacked him in the back of the head with his gun. GoGetta fell to the floor, knocked out. The Russians began to tie him up with rope and some duct tape.

GoGetta became a while later and quickly realized he was tied to a chair. He started to scream and felt thick tape holding his mouth closed.

"Yo Rolo," he heard behind him. "Sleeping Beauty finally woke up."

Rolo walked over to GoGetta with Mikey Fingaz by his side. Mikey snapped his fingers and a Russian soldier ripped the duct tape from GoGetta's mouth.

"So I know you're wondering why you are here in front of me, correct?" Mikey walked a circle around the chair. "Look, let me get straight to the point. Where is your friend Bandz at?" Mikey took one more loop around the chair and then backhanded GoGetta in the mouth, splitting his lip. "Before you answer, think very hard."

Mikey glared down at GoGetta, waited a few seconds, then began to lose his patience. "You and Bandz killed my brother-in-law, didn't you! Or was it somebody else with Bandz?"

"Yo fuck you! I ain't got shit to say to you crackers!" GoGetta spit out a wad of blood at Mikey's face.

Role stepped forward and cracked GoGetta in the jaw with a vicious right hook. He didn't appreciate any disrespectful words towards his boss. GoGetta flinched, but was getting numb to all the abuse directed his way.

"I'm going to ask you one more time about your friend Bandz. I already seen his social media pages and the photos of you two hanging out together." Mikey rubbed his two hands together and looked down.

"I don't know where he lives at now. He moved a few weeks ago."

"So what's his phone number? Give me something here. Help me and help yourself in the process!" Mikey was getting agitated.

"Suck my dick pussy. I ain't helping you with shit!" GoGetta spit out another gob of blood.

"I will be the one who gets the last laugh, asshole." Mikey wiped the blood off of his face with a handkerchief and walked away.

"Kill him," Rolo stated.

The two large Russians stepped forward and grabbed two cans of gasoline from the floor. They opened them and began drenching GoGetta with gas from head to toe. He tried to free himself from the chair, frantically pulling at the ropes but they were tied too tightly.

When the gas was emptied, Mikey Fingaz stepped forward, lighter in hand. "You can clearly see I ain't playing around. All I got to say is tell my brother-in-law hi from me when you see him." He lit the lighter and threw it in GoGetta's lap.

GoGetta instantly burst into flames. Every inch of his body was on fire, and the smell of burning flesh engulfed the house. "Ahh! Ahhhh! Bitch-ass nigga fuck you!"

The Russians watched as GoGetta was burned alive. One thing was for sure: GoGetta had lived out the tattoo he had on his chest. "Death B4 Dishonor." Never would he give up one of his homies.

As the chilling screams from GoGetta stopped, Mikey Fingaz and his crew left the crime scene. Rolo laughed hysterically at all the violence that had occurred. He was a fanatic to anything gruesome.

At the same time, Mikey was deep in thought. His son's recent arrest currently dominated his thoughts.

* * *

Meanwhile on the island...

"We found out who killed my father!" Amber stared at Alex in the visiting room at Riker's. "Do you remember that guy I robbed in the club? You slapped me and gave me back his phone? Well, I went into his phone and found your dad's gambling spot in his photo gallery."

64

"What the hell? Who was this guy?" Alex leaned forward in his chair.

"It was this Blood dude named Bandz. Uncle Mikey has been looking everywhere for him."

As the two talked, they didn't realize that Soulchild was listening in from the seat beside them. Alex was one of the only white guys on 6 South and he stuck out like a sore thumb. The majority of inmates on Riker's were Spanish and black.

Soulchild recognized the name Bandz from Red's stories. He continued to listen to Alex and Amber's conversation to get as much intel as he could to tell Red.

Soulchild made it his business to keep Alex close to him on the unit when they got back. He also told one of his little homies, C-Hood, to make sure Red sent someone up to visit him soon urgently.

CHAPTER 9

It was raining out and a sea of black umbrellas hung outside St. Raymond's Church. GoGetta's funeral packed the church to its capacity. So many people came to pay their respects you would have thought a celebrity had passed away. The inside of the church was dark and gloomy, matching the spirit of the day itself. So many people couldn't believe GoGetta was gone. Both Red and Bandz tried to think of who could have murdered him.

The loss of their comrade had their thoughts in complete disarray. Losing one of Red's best friends drove him to a point of no return. He could imagine so many different sceneries and suspects, but none of them truly made sense to him.

"We are gathered here today to celebrate the life of Jose Santos, AKA GoGetta," the pastor began, looking somberly at the crowd. "He was a bright young man and everyone in the community loved him. It's always sad to see someone so close to us die such a horrible death. Not only will we talk about how he died, and why he died - we will also talk about how he lived. His memory will live on through all of us." At the end of his monologue, the pastor put his right fist up in the air.

GoGetta's mother, Carmen, broke down at this and began to cry hysterically. Red put an arm around her shoulder to show his comfort and give a sense of security.

After the pastor's brief speech, a loud round of applause broke out. The audience consisted of his immediate family and about 200 Neighborhood Gangstas.

Carmen just wouldn't stop crying. Not only was her only child dead, she couldn't even have an open casket service. GoGetta had been burnt to a crisp when homicide finally retrieved his body. Even the funeral parlor's most talented people couldn't make him presentable to show the public. Instead, everyone said their last goodbyes to the photo on top of his casket.

After the pastor spoke, the congregation lined up to pay their final respects. Red ushered Carmen to the front of the church and helped her stay strong as she received hugs and condolences.

All of a sudden the two oak doors of the church

came crashing down. Everyone looked towards the entrance, and ducked behind pews upon seeing the two masked gunmen.

BLATT- BLATT - BLATT - BLATT - BLATT -

The gunmen fired round after round from their AK-47s into the church, scanning around for Bandz. They unleashed bullet after bullet in a torrent of gunfire while they searched.

Both Red and Bandz had taken cover behind the casket at the front of the church. Red retrieved his black SAR 9-mil and began exchanging bullets with the assailants. B-Money and Ammo drew their weapons as well and aimed at the intruders.

- BOOM - BOOM - BOOM -
-BLOCKA - BLOCKA BLOCKA -

Innocent bystanders went down everywhere you looked. The entire church was in a frenzy. All you could hear were the gunshots and screams echoing through the walls. One shot from B-Money hit a shooter in the lower abdomen, dropping the assailant down to one knee.

The congregation knew that bullets don't have eyes or names on them.

Some continued to hide behind the church pews, while others took shelter anywhere they could find hiding spot.

Even though Roses was sour, she still had hope for her and Red. She told Amber that she knew Bandz had killed her father. She never mentioned anything about Red. That's why Mikey sent two of his most trustworthy soldiers to complete the mission. With Roses and Amber plotting against him while working together at Show Palace-, Bandz knew he had God on his side. It just wasn't his time to go.

- BLOCKA - BLOCKA - BLOCKA -
- BLATT - BLATT -

Shell casings of every size and flavor littered the aisles. A bullet from Ammo's .380 pierced the second gunman in the shoulder and his AK-47 sprayed wildly in the air. At this, two more bullets crashed into his chest and forehead. He dropped instantly to the ground.

Police sirens could be heard approaching rapidly. The local precinct was located only a few blocks away from the war zone. On their arrival, there were already two people dead, five wounded, and a stunned crowd.

Ammo had killed one of the two shooters while the other one fled from the scene. Red, along with all the other Neighborhood Gangstas that had discharged their guns, vacated the premises.

Mikey Fingaz had got the drop on the funeral arrangements due to an inside source. The $10,000 reward money for information on Bandz worked in his favor. Money talks and bullshit walks.

Since the incident with Red and Indiana, Roses had been sour. She was the one who had given Mikey the information for the cash. One thing about life though, people are just living to die...

* * *

Two days later...

"Ayo fam why the fuck you touching that phone?" J.C. asked Alex. "That's a Crip phone right there cuz."

"Man I'm just trying to call my lawyer. I don't want no problems." Alex backed off and put his hands off the phone.

Soulchild saw the exchange and stepped over to intervene. "Loc let him use the phone so he can handle his business. He good with me." Soulchild turned to Alex and gestured for him to go ahead. Then he walked away and into the T.V. room.

Waiting for him there stood Golden Child, the head Latin King; Stay Fly, the head YG; Dommi, the head Trini; and Bloodshed, the head Blood.

"Our plan is coming together," Soulchild began. "Once he gets off the phone, we have to set off this race riot."

Stay Fly nodded. "Aight then let's get this done bro." He was anxious to put in some work.

After Red had gotten the message that Soulchild needed to speak with him, Roses had come to visit the Island. Roses told Soulchild that the Russians wanted the head Neighborhood Gangstas abolished for a few acts they committed. Soulchild took Roses information, along with the info from Alex' visit, and designed a plan to benefit Red.

Alex got off the phone and made his way into the bathroom. In the brief time it took him to piss, the unit became a dangerous riot.

Alex walked out of the bathroom and saw fists, chairs, and other blunt objects being thrown by every person in the unit. He turned around and ran back into the bathroom, not realizing that was exactly the wrong move to make.

Soulchild and Stay Fly were hidden inside the bathroom stalls. As soon as they saw Alex walk back in and lean against the bathroom mirror, they charged him with homemade shanks in their hands.

Alex' eyes grew as big as golf balls as he saw two ten-inch blades headed his way. He had never before been in a situation of this magnitude.

Soulchild's first swing plunged deep into Alex' right cheekbone, and he drew back in pain.

"Ahh! Ahh!" Alex screamed. "Please, man!

Whatever you want I'll do!"

Stay Fly ignored him and swung his knife into Alex' jugular vein. Blood spurted everywhere and Alex tried to staunch the bleeding with both of his hands.

The two continued to poke more holes in Alex than a Jamaican tank top.

In less than thirty seconds, they must have stabbed him more than thirty times. Blood splattered everywhere in the bathroom.

Soulchild put up a hand. "You smell that? I think that nigga shitted himself. Let's get the fuck out of here before the C.O.s come storming in." He wiped off the weapons and put them back in the stash spot.

Blood, piss, and shit ran down the bathroom drain as Alex laid on the floor, bleeding out. Soulchild and Stay Fly made their way back into the dorm area.

"Everybody get down on the fucking floor! Face first!" the captain screamed, pointing the beanbag gun at random inmates.

The two had made it out of the bathroom just in time. There had to be at least 30 C.O.s dressed up in full riot gear - helmets, shields, and all.

Two inmates ignored the C.O.s and continued to exchange blows with each other until the O-C gas began to spray.

The majority of inmates laid on their stomach,

awaiting the next order. People started covering their eyes and mouths, as the gas had everyone coughing and tearing.

After a couple minutes, windows began to open to let out some of the gas.

"Okay now. Everyone stand up and line up. We are doing a body search." One C.O. gestured towards the far wall.

One by one, the inmates took off their shirts, showed their hands, and had their bodies scanned for any marks or bruises. The C.O.s were looking for tell-tale signs of fighting.

Stay Fly didn't even notice the blood specs scattered around his white t-shirt. As he handed over his shirt to the C.O., it was noticed and the captain came over. After a brief conversation, they told Stay Fly to put his hands behind his back to cuff up.

Soulchild watched dumbfounded as they escorted Stay Fly to the box. Stay Fly looked back. "Yo we good son! You already know G's."

* * *

Four days later...

Cathy warmed up a chicken sandwich in a microwave in the C.O. break room. As she waited for it to heat through, she overheard a conversation Captain Dumont was having on his cell phone.

"I was checking on your son making sure he was good. I'm sorry for your loss. But from my investigation and information from my in-house rats, the Bloods were behind this."

Captain Dumont assumed the Bloods had ordered the hit because they were the biggest gang in the facility. They were behind all the drugs, slashings, and most of the violence.

Captain Dumont was also on Mikey Fingaz' payroll. Even though he didn't have any solid facts, he felt like he needed an answer for him.

No one was ever charged for Alex Kujovich's homicide. There were no witnesses and no weapons related to the incident were ever found.

Mikey Fingaz was infuriated by his son's death. He was disappointed he hadn't gotten him out of there sooner, trying to teach him a lesson instead.

In response, Mikey declared war on the Bloods as a collective whole.

He spread the word around the Russian mob and even sent for some of Moscow's finest killers. Mikey knew that in order to win this battle a lot of bodies were gonna have to drop. The Bloods were the most dominant gang in New York City at that time.

While Captain Dumont continued to talk on his cell phone, Cathy texted Red. She told him they had to get up after her shift was over. She had to put Red on to what she heard and make sure he was on point. Cathy knew a bit more due to her pillow talk with the captain after their sexcapades.

Red was family. She had to keep his best interests at heart and make sure nothing bad happened to her favorite cousin.

* * *

Two weeks later...

Mikey Fingaz ordered Rolo and his army to invade any hood he thought was controlled by Bloods. Mikey didn't know the difference between sets - he called all Bloods Blood. All he wanted was payback for his brother-in-law's and son's deaths. He was on a mission and wasn't stopping until Bandz was dead and enough members of the Bloods were with him.

"There he goes right there!" Mikey Fingaz pointed to Bandz. He stood by the corner store with a group of other Bloods.

Rolo had half of his body out the window and his AR-15 pointed at the group of gang bangers.

-    BLATT - BLATT - BLATT - BLATT -

Rolo hit two Bloods in the crowd and Bandz ducked behind a truck. He pulled out his Tec 9 and returned fire to the car.

- BLOCKA BLOCKA - BLOCKA -

Bandz hit one of the tires and watched as the car swerved wildly. More shots came at Bandz from a second vehicle with more Russians. They had been riding through neighborhoods five cars deep, looking for action. This time was no different.

Two bullets hit Bandz. One hit in his right arm and the other ripped flesh from his left shoulder. As Bandz held his arm, he heard a parade of bullets fly at the bodega on the corner. Already three of his homies were stretched out on the street.

The cars moved on, and eventually Mikey Fingaz learned that Bandz was a Neighborhood Gangsta. A blood named Sha Banga told him that Bandz claimed a West Coast set and East Coast sets don't really fuck with them like that. He also revealed main areas the Neighborhood Gangstas were located at.

It was crazy how this gang world worked. In reality, every Blood ain't your blood.

CHAPTER 10

Razor started off his bid at a United States Penitentiary in Lee County and ended up stabbing a mid-west dude 15 times in the face for beating him in a dice game with no money. That stabbing landed him in the notorious S.M.U. program, or Special Management Unit. The unit was in Colorado and housed the most violent and disruptive individuals throughout the Bureau of Prisons.

Razor had been wildin out since he had been in. He spread the Neighborhood Gangstas throughout the entire B.O.P. and brought home some of the most official people he ran across. They were in every penitentiary from USP Pollock to USP Hazelton.

After 18 months of being in the box in the S.M.U.

program, he ended up getting shipped out to Inez, Kentucky to USP Big Sandy.

Razor was excited to hear about leaving. Being in a cell for 23 hours a day and only one hour of recreation was definitely taking its toll on him. The S.M.U. program was a step-down program. It was only one step away from ADX Colorado, which is the SuperMax facility.

Finally the day came and Razor left Florence, CO to go to USP Big Sandy. All the stories he had heard about the prison had him on point.

After going through R&D procedures like stripping out, getting finger-printed, getting interviewed by C.O.s and taking I.D. photos, he was ready to walk the compound.

Razor tucked his bedroll under his right arm and strolled down the long corridor to his unit C-4. Suddenly he noticed a familiar face.

"What's up Blood? Long time no see homie!" Razor threw up the "B" at the bounty hunter D-Mack. Him and D-Mack had run the Blood car together over at USP Lee County before Razor went to the program.

"Damn Blood! What unit they got you going to, fool?"

"They told me C-4, Blood." Razor continued to walk by different units, looking at the writing on the walls.

"Homie you coming to my unit don't trip. It's only

5 Damu's on our unit. You got D-L from Pueblo Bishops, Ryder from Sex Money Murder, Kapone from Neighborhood Piru, and Tyke from G-Shine."

They finally arrived to the door to the unit. Today everybody knew that the bus arrived. It came every two weeks with new arrivals so a bunch of people came to the window to see who had pulled up. Razor and D-Mack waited for the C.O. to open the door.

"Can I have your I.D. sir?" The C.O. opened up the door and let them in the unit.

People stopped playing chess, watching T.V., or doing whatever they were doing to get a good look at Razor. He saw a few familiar faces he had known from other spots.

After checking in with the C.O., D-Mack took him to his cell. Razor ended up bunking with Kapone, the Neighborhood Piru homie from Inglewood, California.

After dropping off his bedroll, Razor met all the Blood homies on the unit. They gave him a mesh bag filled with hygiene, food, and clothes until he got his property. Since it was almost nine o'clock lock-in, Razor and Kapone were talking in front of their cell when out of nowhere, a bald Spanish guy was stabbed.

Razor turned to look, and saw a dark-skinned cat with braids plunging a metal knife into the Spanish guy's face and chest repeatedly.

"Work call! Work call niggas!" he shouted for all to hear.

C.O.s came running from all areas. "Lock in! Lock in now!" one of them yelled.

Razor and Kapone got in their cell before they started to spray gas. After closing the door, Razor looked out the glass and stared expressionless at the scene in front of him.

After the C.O. locked the cell door, Razor brushed his teeth and made his bed to lay down. He was tired from the jet lag and bus ride to Kentucky. The transit in the Feds was vicious.

Razor got in his bed, staring at the ceiling until his eyes got heavy and he drifted off to sleep.

* * *

A few days later...

Razor settled into USP Big Sandy. He had seen a bunch of familiar faces from his travels through the system. One person he had known well for over a decade was Diablo, a Black Hand in the Mexican Mafia. They had been together back in the 90's in Pelican Bay. They had history with each other and built a solid rapport.

Diablo controlled the black tar heroin trade throughout the entire compound. It cost $1,000 for a street gram in Big Sandy.

Razor knew that once Jennifer came up there, he could flood the compound with all the exotic bud. Jennifer was riding with Razor so far during his incarceration. She had brought him plenty of balloons while he was in USP Lee County. They made a ton of money together and she would do anything for him. Even behind bars, their relationship was still unbreakable. Plus, Red used to send him money out of the kitty every month, so he stood straight financially.

"Razor come outside with me to the yard and walk a couple laps." Diablo tied up his black Nike Cortez sneakers and looked at Razor.

It was a rarity to find Mexicans walk with blacks on the yard. Especially no Mexican Mafia. They usually stick with their own kind.

As Razor and Diablo walked the yard together, Diablo had three Surenos behind them as security. There were quite a few whispers as to why a black and a Mexican were laughing and walking together. United States Penitentiaries were real segregated when it came to race.

"Look my friend, I told you to walk the yard with me to ask for your assistance. I know you have a voice with the Bloods. I know how you conduct your gang and run it with a velvet glove around an iron fist." Diablo stopped walking and parked himself on a bench. "Your homie D-L, owes me a few thousand dollars."

Razor sat down next to Diablo. "How long has he owed you this money? And have you spoken to any other Bloods besides me about it?"

"It's been two months now. You're the only person I talked to besides D-L about this." Diablo slowly stroked his goatee.

"Aight Diablo. Once my property gets here and I show my paperwork, I'll make that situation right. I got you dog."

"OK that's fair. I respect that." Diablo extended his right hand for a handshake. "Now that we are past that, I have a proposition for you. If I can rely on anyone, it's you."

The two spoke a bit longer until it was yard recall and they had to return to the unit. After all those years, Diablo still hadn't changed one bit. Razor knew that the two of them together could build something great.

* * *

Back in 1992, Razor was housed in Pelican Bay, home of the most violent and infamous gangstas throughout the state of California. Razor was young, wild, and had a fresh ten years to do.

This day, he was doing pull-ups with a group of Bloods out in the yard. He saw an Aryan Brotherhood dude named Jordan go into a Mexican Mafia stash spot. He took a shank from under the bleachers, looked around, and then walked away. Razor saw the actual theft taking place, and in prison, stealing was the worst thing you could do.

"Ayo fool, that mark-ass busta Jordan stole from the Mexicans." Razor turned to his Blood homie Taco, doing reps on the pull-up bar.

Taco was half black and half Mexican, spoke fluent Spanish, and mingled with both crowds. Taco's cousin Flaco was also the head Mexican Mafia on the compound.

With so much tension between races, any incident could spark a race riot instantly. Razor just shook his head side to side as he saw Jordan stuff the shank in his waistband and walk away.

That night, Taco was walking with his cousin to dinner, when he told him about the theft.

Flaco turned to him and stopped. "Don't play with me - you serious?" How the hell you know it was him?"

"One of my Blood homies saw him take it while we were doing pull-ups in the yard." Taco looked around the chow hall, but figured Razor was cooking something in the unit instead.

The next afternoon, Razor was sitting at a table in the yard, playing chess. He looked up to see Taco and Flaco walking across the basketball court together towards him.

Taco walked up first. "What's brackin Blood? My relative trying to speak with you."

"Hey Razor. I want you to confirm what Taco said. Did Jordan steal one of our knives from the bleachers?" Flaco stared Razor straight in the eyes, looking for signs of deceit.

"Yeah. I seen him take it and put it in his waistband."

"Okay. I'm asking you to do me a favor. I want you to stand on that in front of my two comrades and the head of the A-B's, Hammer."

Razor nodded. "Aight then, I know what I saw. And knowing these prison politics, sneak-thieving is forbidden. Let's handle this then." Razor loosened the string that his knife was attached to on his pants, stood up, and followed the two.

Flaco, Razor, and Taco walked up to a group of Mexicans by the handball courts. In the middle of the crowd stood Diablo and Bobby: the other two Black Hands in the prison. The three head Mexicans went off to converse privately, and after about ten minutes they walked back over.

Diablo gestured towards the baseball field. "Come on. Let's go see Hammer. He over there on the bleachers by the field."

The five of them walked towards Hammer as many prisoners looked on in suspense. As they walked, Razor's heart pounded with each step. He didn't know how this was going to play out, but knew it would all be a part of God's plan.

Hammer saw the five approach and automatically

stood up from the bleacher. Hammer was huge. He stood 6'5", had blond hair, blue eyes, a muscular build, and a swastika tatted on his left cheek right under his eye. He was completely no-nonsense, and ran the Aryan Brotherhood in Pelican Bay. Hammer always stood on what was right. His motto was, "There's no right way to do wrong."

"What's up my friend?" Flaco extended his right hand to greet Hammer."

"What can I do for you Flaco?" Hammer asked, looking at Taco and Razor from head to toe.

"Well, there's a major issue. One of your brothers stole one of our weapons yesterday." Flaco looked over and gave Jordan a menacing stare.

Jordan had fear written all over his face. He thought he was discreet when he took the shank.

"Oh yeah?" Hammer asked. "Well who took your weapon Flaco?"

"It was Jordan who took it. You know I never make accusations unless they are true."

Jordan overheard the conversation and immediately turned bright red. "That's a lie! You're gonna believe this wetback brother?"

Razor wasted no time and sprung into action. He ripped his knife from the string and started swinging it wildly at Jordan, puncturing his left hand and shoulder.

- BOOM - BOOM -

Shots were fired from the gun tower 'as live rounds were fired to stop the incident.

Suddenly everyone drew their weapons. Diablo ended up getting stabbed by Hammer, but Jordan got injured badly and almost died.

From that day on, Diablo would never forget Razor. He respected him for standing on his word and having no fear. They created a life-long bond that both would remember.

CHAPTER 11

Between the Bloods and the Russian mob, pandemonia ruled the streets of New York City. The N.Y.P.D. had their hands full and were really earning their checks. Plus, the funeral parlors were getting rich off this war. There were so many bodies dropping and someone had to take care of them.

Red had so much running through his mind lately. The only thing keeping him calm was the Grand Daddy Kush he smoked. Plus, his Green Bay Packers were beating Minnesota 34-16 on his flat screen.

"Hey baby," Indiana called from the kitchen. "I got something to tell you."

Red pushed the mute button on the remote and turned around to see Indiana walk into the living room in a red bra and thong.

"We are having a baby! I just took another

pregnancy test and it came up positive. I haven't had my period and was throwing up the past three mornings." Indiana had a huge smile plastered across her face as she walked over to the couch.

Red sat still as her words echoed in his mind. "Are you serious ma?" He knew it could be true. He and Indiana never used condoms and he always nutted inside her.

Indiana frowned. "You seem like you ain't happy or something." She put both hands on her hips and twisted her lips.

Red grinned and grabbed at her body. "Come here sexy! You look good as hell when you getting mad." As he played with Indiana, his mind drifted into the forbidden. He thought about the lifestyle he led.

In Red's heart he knew it wasn't a good time to bring a baby into the world. Red didn't want to feel responsible if something were to happen to the baby amidst all this chaos. All he could think about was how bold the Russians were getting and how they got the drop on his set.

* * *

Days later...

Red and B-Money were inside, rolling dice and taking everybody's money in Cee-Lo while the block was deserted. It was 4 am, a mild summer night, and the dope boys were earning their living.

At first Red came by just to drop off a few pounds of Girl scout cookies for B-Money, but when he walked in and saw the packed hallway it looked like Las Vegas had come to the hood. Amongst the familiar faces, the one that got the most attention was Roses. She rocked a white Chanel catsuit, and dripped sex from every pore in her body.

Red hadn't had sex with her since he had been dating Indiana. One thing about Red was that he wore loyalty like a badge of honor.

"Yo Roses come here. Let me speak to you outside real quick." After Red won a few games, he pointed towards the door.

Roses licked her lips seductively and strutted towards him like a model on the runway. She thought Red had finally come to his senses and decided to leave Indiana.

Red shut the door behind them and looked Roses in the eyes. "Look. You know I will always fuck with you no matter what, but stop letting your emotions override your thinking. Apple told me that slick comment you said about my wifey."

Roses folded her arms across her chest. "Yeah I said Red lost his mind fucking with that weird looking bitch. So what? Red, at the end of the day I love you and my, loyalty been with you for years since we were little. The only reason I came home

89

was because of you! Why are you doing me like this?" she demanded.

Red sighed. "I understand everything you just told me. I just can't see myself settling down with a woman living the same lifestyle I'm involved in." Red opened his mouth to continue, but just then a black BMW X6 screeched to a halt at the curb.

As a natural reaction, Red slid his chrome .357 out of his pants and Roses pulled out her .22 from the Chanel bag. There was so much drama in the hood lately and Red couldn't afford to slip up.

Red approached the truck with his weapon armed and ready. The driver-side window slid down and Red's little homie Flashy peeked out.

"N's up Blood! What's brackin with you? I need like an ounce of bud." Flashy smiled and turned down the volume on the console, which was blasting Big Deal's new mixtape 'Feeding the Streetz.'

Just then the back window slid down and Amber appeared. "Hey bitch, why you ain't come to work tonight?"

Roses looked over at Amber. "I ain't feel like it tonight. I been dancing in there for months non-stop." She held out her arms, waiting for a hug from her friend.

Amber hopped out of the truck with her friend Climax. The three hugged and kissed each other on the cheeks. Red stared lustily at Amber, as this was only the third time he ever seen her.

Bandz spotted Amber get out of the car and hopped down off the stoop.

"Blood! That's shorty who booked me for my phone, money, and cigarettes at the club that night!" Bandz limped slightly and grabbed his crutches off the railing.

Amber squinted her eyes, trying to get a good look at Bandz' face. After the Russians had come through, Red's little homies had shot out most of the street lights on the block.

Even though she couldn't clearly make out Bandz' face, she recognized his voice instantly and began to panic. Her initial thought was to run, but she knew that Roses was there to back her up. In Amber's mind she thought she could talk her way out of this.

Red pointed his gun at Amber. "So you are the thief that stole my homie's stuff, huh?"

Amber's heart beat faster and faster and her mind raced. "I thought he was this other guy that came to the club one night and gave me $1,000 in counterfeit ones."

Roses felt stunned. "Damn girl. I ain't know that you robbed one of my homies at the club."

Climax glanced up from her phone. "You know we been robbing and pulling tricks there for the longest."

"Yo Blood, it's all coming to me now." Bandz

approached the truck and leaned on the hood. "I knew I seen that bitch somewhere else before!"

Red nodded. "Yeah you just said she was the bitch in the club that robbed your dumb ass."

"Nah, nah. I know exactly where I remember her from. Right Amber?" Bandz raised an eyebrow.

Amber grew petrified and started shaking in her red bottoms. She avoided all eye contact and didn't know what was about to come next.

Bandz looked at Red. "I got places to go and people to kill. That's shorty from the gambling spot!"

Red's eyes grew wide. "The Russian joint!" He immediately shot Amber right in the chest, dropping her to the ground.

Then Red turned his gun on Climax, shooting her three times in the head and killing her instantly. Glancing back, he saw Amber still alive and crawling on the ground, trying to get away.

Amber grabbed Roses' leg. "You gonna let them do this to me Roses? You know my uncle ain't gonna let y'all get away with this." Blood dripped from the corners of her mouth.

Roses pointed her gun down and dumped two bullets right into Amber's skull, killing her. "Blood rule bitch."

Residents from the neighborhood looked out their windows, being nosey. Red had to make moves quickly before someone reported it to the police. "Put these bitches in the back seat Blood."

Red dragged Climax by her hair towards the truck as Flashy got out and helped his big homie. After they laid Amber's body on top of Climax in the back, they fled the scene and jumped on the Cross-Bronx Expressway.

Flashy banged his fist on the steering wheel. "Damn Blood, you fucked up my after party! I was thirsty to fuck them hoes. I spent wild bread already tonight!"

Red busted out laughing. "Homie it's a million bad bitches in the world you have plenty more to choose from."

Roses had stayed back on the block to keep Red posted about any police sightings and gather up information from the neighbors.

Red knew two things about the hood someone always sees something and someone is always talking. Red made their first stop to dump his gun in the Hudson River. He originally wanted to tie bricks to Amber's and Climax' bodies, but thought of an even better plan. One that would make a bold statement.

"Ayo Skrap - type in 2314 Bronxdale Ave." Red glanced back and shook his head at the two dead bodies. He knew what would cause the most impact to his new Russian friends.

About a half hour later they arrived at their destination: one of Mikey Fingaz' restaurants. Red had seen it in a manilla folder Indiana kept at the crib. Red hopped out of the truck, opened up the passenger door, then looked both ways up and down the block. When the coast was clear he pulled Amber by her legs out of the back seat.

The only sound was a loud thud as Amber's head dropped on the pavement. Flashy threw the truck in park and hopped out to help with Climax' body.

Red gestured at Flashy. "Fuck Climax. Come here and grab Amber's arms while I grab her legs and swing her body with me." They picked up the body and prepared to swing. "On the count of three we gonna throw her body through the glass window. One... Two... Three!'"

The two threw Amber's body at the window. It broke and glass shattered everywhere.

"Come on hurry up! Let's do the same thing with Climax' body as well." Red grabbed her ankles while Flashy grabbed her arms and they threw it on top of Amber.

Flashy looked hurriedly down the block. "Let's dip big bro." He ran back to the driver's seat and started the engine.

Red nodded, but first grabbed a can of spray paint from his back pocket.

He sprayed "Blood Rules" on the door to the restaurant, hopped in the truck, and they peeled out from the block without anyone ever knowing they had been there.

* * *

It was 8 am and the restaurant manager Brittany arrived to open up as she always did every morning. As she walked up to the door, she noticed that damn near the entire front window was gone and glass was scattered about the sidewalk. Then she noticed the spray paint over the door and didn't know what to expect. Brittany peeked into the window, then let out a chilling scream at the sight within.

The first thing she saw was Amber's dead body laid across the floor.

It brought tears to her eyes. She had known Amber all her life. Brittany pulled out her phone to dial 911, but then remembered Mikey Fingaz' words to her:

"No matter what happens, always call me first before you do anything."

Instead, she dialed Mikey. After the fourth ring, FaceTime connected the two.

"Yes?" Mikey answered. "Is everything okay, Brittany?"

"No! Look at this right here." Brittany flipped the screen to show Amber's and Climax' bodies sprawled across the floor.

Mikey almost dropped the phone in surprise as he saw the horrific scene that his niece witnessed.

CHAPTER 12

Later that week...

"Listen up y'all! I had to call this emergency meeting because so many things have been happening lately." Red paused for a moment and looked out at the 300 or so members of Neighborhood Gangstas that stood in front of him. He knew right then and there that every move was critical. Any bad decision at this point would affect them all and things were already spiraling out of control.

Homies from all five boroughs were present in the park as Red continued. "Between some of us getting shot up on the block and them Russians shooting up GoGetta's funeral, there's been a lot of disrespect towards our set and I ain't feeling all that." Red scanned the crowd seriously, looking at each and every face.

Red thought back about the conversation he had with Flashy earlier that same day. That conversation had directly led to him calling this meeting. Flashy told him that Climax was fucking Sha Banga and he bragged about how the Russian mob was going to wipe out, Neighborhood Gangstas and then the 1 8 Trey Niggas would take over.

It made Red angry now, just thinking about it. He knew right then and there what he was going to tell the set.

Red paused, rubbing his goatee with his right hand as he considered the crowd in front of him. "It's lit with the Russians and them 1 8 Trey Niggas. It's time to put on for the hood. Soo wooooo!" Red threw the neighborhood sign in the air and stared at his homies.

* * *

Meanwhile in Brooklyn, Mikey Fingaz looked around the room at the collection of comrades seated around his table. "Let me get everyone's attention for a moment. We have a real problem on our hands." He pounded the table with his fist, making the empty shot glasses of vodka jump. "These fucking scumbags have got real close to home. I want each and every Blood killed by the time the sun rises. One of the little pricks Sha told me that we're at war with one specific section called the Neighborhood Gangstas."

Once Mikey's niece had been murdered, he immediately contacted Moscow for more soldiers to help him. The Bloods were the deepest gang in New York City and in order to prevail he needed as much assistance as he was able to get.

"Don't worry boss," Rolo replied confidently. "We will annihilate those Neighborhood Gangstas or whatever they call themselves. No one will ever disrespect the Kujovich Dynasty!" As he spoke he made sure to catch eyes with each of the 20 people in the room.

There was only one thing on everyone's mind: the second they saw the color red, they were gonna start shooting. Period. Nothing would stop them until their revenge was complete.

CHAPTER 13

Bandz reclined in a red leather chair in the living room and continued demolishing some honey BBQ wings. He was about halfway through the latest episode of Power when the doorbell rang. He glanced at the clock. Almost midnight. No one just comes by the apartment without letting him know first.

Bandz sat up, loaded his .380, and sauntered over to the door. As he glanced through the peephole he saw Roses standing there, waiting for him. He unlatched the chains, opened the door, and watched as she just strutted past him and plopped down on the couch.

"Yo Roses what's poppin? Why you rollin up to my crib at this time un-announced?" Bandz closed the door and looked back at Roses, his eyes scrolling back and forth from her thighs to her breasts. He had always had a thing for her ever since they were little kids.

"My fault Blood, but what I just saw on Red's Instagram blew my mind.

He posted a photo of two hands. Both had wedding bands on them." As she spoke, tears formed in her eyes and dripped down her face. "Please tell me there ain't no truth to that right there."

Bandz sighed. "Yo Red did tell me yesterday that he was gonna propose to his shorty, so he might have already popped the question." He walked over to the couch, gently patted Roses' back, and took a seat next to her on the couch.

Roses closed her eyes, breathed in deep, then wiped some of the tears from her face. "Do you have a drink in here? I need a shot of some type of liquor."

Bandz nodded, stood up, and made his way to the liquor cabinet. He opened it, grabbed a bottle of Henny, then made his way back to sit next to Roses. She spotted the bottle and quickly snatched it from his hands, popping the top and chugging the expensive liquid. When she came up for air, Bandz noticed a different type of look in her eyes.

"Do you think I'm pretty Bandz?" Roses stood up and spun around to show off her body. "Do you think that bitch Indiana looks better than me?"

Bandz' eyes got wide as he admired every curve

God created on Roses. She continued.to twirl around, then tripped and fell over right in Bandz lap. His dick was rising by the second and she was making him horny as hell. He decided to make a move, grabbed Roses chin with his left hand and kissed her on the lips. To his surprise she kissed him back passionately.

Roses straddled his lap and began to slide her hands up his t-shirt and all over his stomach. She grinded into his lap as their tongues started fighting for control.

Bandz reached up and grabbed her breast through her shirt and realized she wasn't wearing a bra. He immediately ripped up her shirt, exposing her perky titties, and put his mouth on the right one: sucking on it like a newborn baby would.

Roses moaned gently, and stopped him after a few seconds. She got up and started peeling off all her clothes. As she did that, Bandz took off his jeans and boxers but kept his shirt on. Roses finished and looked down at Bandz, her eyes growing wide at his huge erection.

Roses dropped to her knees and began attacking his rock-hard manhood with her hands, mouth, and tongue. She wrapped her right hand around his dick while she sucked his balls into her mouth. Saliva dripped all over his lap onto the couch. Her head game was top-notch.

After a few minutes of that, Roses wrapped her

full lips around his pulsing rod and made the entire thing disappear into her mouth. Bandz was beyond ecstatic at what was happening. He threw his head back while Roses sucked him off and let her do her thing.

Soon, Roses began to speed up and started to gag on his manhood. The sounds of her slurps had Bandz wide open. She took his dick out of her mouth because she didn't want to spoil the moment and have him nut too fast.

Instead, Roses decided to straddle Bandz and ride his dick. He slid inside her tight, slippery vagina. He closed his eyes tight as her pussy lips wrapped around his manhood like a hand in a glove. She started bouncing up and down on his lap, taking every single inch of his penis.

"Oh yeah!" Bandz cried. "Damn this feels so good!" He matched her motions and thrusted fast and hard inside of her. Roses' breasts were jiggling in his face with every thrust.

"Uh, uh, uh, oh my god!" Roses screamed loudly as she was about to cum.

Bandz was sweating as he kept long-stroking inside of her. He took a handful of her hair, pulled it back and started digging even deeper. A few more pumps took him to ectasy as he squirted all inside Roses.

She landed on top of him drained, but feeling much better. After Bandz dumped his load of semen in her she just rolled over next to him on the couch.

"Ayo Roses that pussy is as good as hell. It's almost as good as a bucket of fried chicken from K.F.C." Bandz sat on the sofa naked and laughing.

"I never thought we would reach this point. But I'm feeling you and I been had my eyes on you since we were in school. I always felt I should have picked you instead of Red." Roses stared deep into his eyes. "I thought Razor should have left you in charge. When you gonna be a man and stop being up under Red's ass all the time? You should get your own set!" Roses began to put on her pink panties.

As she got quietly dressed, Bandz sat there and thought about everything she said.

CHAPTER 14

Flashy pulled the car closer to their destination: 183rd and Davidson.

He glanced behind him to make sure that Red and B-Money were locked and loaded. Turning back to the dark streets, he made a left turn and got ready to pull the car over.

"Blood stop the truck right here. Let me get out with B-Money I saw a bunch of them 18 Trey Niggas in front of one of those buildings!" Red threw on his black Champion hoody and got out, 9 mil drawn.

B-Money drew his P-89 Ruger from his waistband and jogged behind Red. As they got closer to the crowd, they ducked behind parked cars to stay un-noticed.

Red locked his eyes on Sha Banga amongst the crowd, then stood up and started firing at him. Out of nowhere a white Lincoln Navigator tried to side-swipe Red as it left a parking space. Red dodged, rolled behind another parked car, and crouched up to re-aim his weapon. At the same time B-Money let off two shots, hitting the driver in the neck and shattering the window. The truck swerved and collided into two smaller cars.

Red peeked over the hood of the car he hid behind and busted off three quick shots. Two pierced random people in the crowd while the third barely missed Sha Banga. People were running and scattered all over the block to avoid getting shot in the crossfire.

Sha Banga took off running in the direction of Flashy's truck. Just as he was about to reach it, he slowed down to try and catch his breath. Flashy saw him and hopped out of the truck with his .40 cal. While Sha was bent over catching his breath, Flashy took the opportunity to shoot him in the head four times, killing him instantly.

- BOOM - BOOM - BOOM - BOOM -

Sha Banga's limp body collapsed to the concrete in a pool of blood. Flashy jogged back to his truck, and a bullet whizzed by his ear. He glanced back and saw a plain-clothes officer pointing a handgun at him.

"Freeze muthafucker! Don't make a move. Put

your hands up now!"

Flashy's initial thought was to run, but instead he pointed his .40 cal at the officer and squeezed three shots off, missing him. A second officer ran towards them shooting, and hit Flashy in his leg and in the back of his head - knocking a chunk of his brain through his forehead.

As Flashy fell to the ground, Red and B-Money were in a gun battle of their own with the 18 Trey Bloods. They heard sirens and saw paddy wagons pull up to the scene. B-Money took off running towards Flashy's truck while Red ran in the opposite direction. Red might have been born and raised in the Bronx, but this hood was unfamiliar to him.

Red ducked off into an alley to escape the female officer hot on his trail. He saw that it was a dead end and looked around for some type of way out.

"You're trapped now!" the officer shouted. "Come out with your hands up!"

"Fuck all that. You gonna have to kill me bitch!"

"Baby is that you?" Indiana recognized Red's voice and looked up from behind the garbage bin she hid behind.

Red was shocked to see his wifey standing in front of him wearing her police uniform.

"Shots fired! Shots fired! Suspect went west-bound on Davidson Ave!"

Indiana yelled into her walkie-talkie, letting off

two shots in the air.

She quickly turned back to Red. "Get the fuck out of here! Go east-bound and take the train and I'll see you back at the crib."

Red jogged in the direction she told him to go, jumped the turnstile at the station, and headed back home. As he sat on the train he prayed that B-Money and Flashy were OK and hadn't become casualties in this war.

* * *

The very next night was cool, crisp, and gentle. Snowflakes dropped softly from the dark clouds above. Jennifer took the train back from her best friend's baby shower. All the talk about babies got her thinking. She flashed back to when her son Red was a little boy. Even thinking about him at that age had her smiling.

"The next stop is Parkchester."

The automated voice snapped Jennifer out of her revelrie and she zipped up her jacket. Once the train came to a halt, she stood up and walked towards the exit on the train platform. As she walked out, two white men followed behind her.

Jennifer was from the hood so she figured these two men were either lost or up to no good. Where she was from, there weren't any white people. The population consisted of all Spanish and blacks.

Other than the three of them, the train station was deserted.

She began to speed up her steps to find out if they were really following her or she was just being paranoid. But her intuition proved correct as one of the men sped up to match her pace.

Jennifer reached into her Coach bag and grabbed a can of mace Indiana had given her. That, along with her trusty switchblade, would stay in her hands as she glanced around for anyone she knew. The apartment was only two blocks away, but she needed friendly faces.

While she stood on the corner waiting to cross the street, she felt a hand grab her shoulder. Jennifer sprung around on a pivot and in one quick motion sprayed the man with the can of mace in her hand.

"Ahn! Ahh! This bitch is crazy!" He grabbed his burning face with both hands.

Before she had a chance to spray any more, the other man lunged at her. He wrapped his muscular arms around her body as she squirmed, kicking wildly trying to get free. A white Cadillac CTS drove up to the curb and two more Russians jumped out.

The only people outside at the time were cab drivers trying to get a fare before the night ended.

"Help me! Help me please!" Jennifer screamed at the top of her lungs as she struggled to break free from the assailants. She kicked one in the balls and he dropped instantly to one knee. The other three dragged her over to the Cadillac as she continued to fight them.

"Leave the lady alone!" A brolic Puerto Rican cab driver walked over to the scene, cracking his knuckles.

The Russians' attention was diverted to the new man on the scene. As their grasp on Jennifer loosened for a second, she took the opportunity to break free and run. Two Russians followed her while two stayed to handle the cab driver.

Jennifer dropped the can of mace earlier, but still had her switchblade. As she ran, she heard five gunshots go off behind her. She had never been no scared-soft chick, but just knowing they had guns frightened her a bit.

A lot of the blocks were one-way, so it wasn't the Cadillac she had to worry about - just the two men chasing her. This was her hood. She was born and raised here and if anyone knew the shortcuts and hideouts it was her.

As she was running and thinking, one of the men caught up to her and tackled her to the ground. Jennifer struggled and tried to break free while there was still only one of them on her. Grabbing the switch-blade from her pocket, she pushed the button to release the blade. With all her might, she swung it at the assailant but he deflected it into her leather purse. With a second swing she plunged it inside one of the man's lungs, puncturing it on impact. As the wind got knocked out of him, so did the fight. The other Russian ran to his comrade's aid and let Jennifer get away.

When she saw they were no longer following, Jennifer dipped off in her homegirl Ginnett's building. She started hitting every buzzer on the wall until someone finally let her in. Jennifer ran to the elevator, mashed the button for the fifth floor, then slid down to the floor to catch her breath. She was paranoid that they knew where she lived and didn't want to risk her capture by going back home.

Her phone was dead and she needed a charge to call Red and warn him. This was one of those times when she missed Razor the most. Not only was he her lover and best friend, but her protector as well.

CHAPTER 15

- RING - RING - RING - RING -

"Yo," Red answered the phone without looking at the screen.

"You have a prepaid call. You will not be charged for this call. This call is from 'Razor', an inmate at a Federal Prison. To accept this call press five, to block this call press 7, to decline this call hang up." Red pressed five as soon as the recording ended.

"What's brackin lil homie how are you doing? I tried to call your mother but she ain't pick up the phone. Is everything good?"

"I'm bickin back as always. So much has been poppin since you been gone. At times I wish you were here. Mama love good." Red sounded tired, irritated, and defeated.

"You're like my son. I know how you move blood. I m gonna drop a jewel on you - many people are ignorant of their true destiny. They strive for things that don't belong to them and would only bring failure and dissatisfaction if attained."

Red sighed. "Damn you know me so well. At times I think what would Razor do if he were in this scenario? But we been beefing hard out here with these Russians. Shit been super lit..."

- CLICK -

In the middle of the sentence, Razor hung up the phone. He wasn't trying to catch any new indictments. He already knew how the government played. The Feds were vicious when it came to using tactics. Especially when Red was being reckless and talking like that. That's just the intel they needed to establish a solid case.

Razor wasn't letting that happen if he had anything to do with it. He knew that if people realized the power of words, they would be more cautious when using them. Many people have brought disaster into their lives through idle words.

* * *

Jennifer charged her phone and finally got in touch with Red. Last night and the failed kidnapping had scarred her mentally. She suggested that Red meet her at their favorite restaurant: Jimbo's on Soundview Ave.

She stood in front of the restaurant with her hands tucked inside the front pouch of her hoodie as she waited for her son to arrive. Down the block Jennifer saw Red diddy-bopping in her direction with a black Polo sweatsuit with black and grey Air Max 95s. He had a slight smirk on his face: the one he always wore when he saw his mother. Red adored his mom and would go through hell on earth for her.

Red gave Jennifer a big bear hug and kissed her on the cheek. They walked into Jimbo's so they could order and get some food. "Table for two please."

The waiter led them to the closest empty table, where they sat down. When Jennifer removed the hood from her hair, Red noticed a scratch right above her right eye. "Yo ma what the hell happened to you?"

Jennifer put her head down and looked at the menu. She looked back up and met her son's eyes, then tried to explain to him what had happened to her the night before.

"Look. I don't know what you are into as of late, but these white men tried to kidnap me from the train station. They tried to abduct me in a white car." As she spoke, tears fell from her eyes and her hands began to tremble slightly.

Red got angrier and angrier as his mother spoke. As soon as she said the words "white men", he knew they were Russian mobsters. But how the fuck did they know who his mom was? How did they know where to catch her? So many questions.

Someone close to him must be playing both sides. But who would do that to him? His entire circle he damn near grew up with.

"...so I maced one of them, kicked one in the balls, and got away to Ginnett's. I'm lucky to be alive - they had guns and everything." Jennifer finished her story and stared at her son from across the table.

Red banged his right fist on the table hard, startling his mom. If this were a cartoon, steam would have been coming out of his ears and nostrils. He was pissed. "Ma, I'm gonna have to let you stay at my house. I don't know if they know where you live, but I'm pretty sure they do."

Red pushed his plate of food away. He had lost his appetite. He ended up just watching his mother eat a hamburger and some fries as he scrolled through Facebook. His curiosity got the best of him and he looked up the name Kujovich. There were a few familiar faces there.

Jennifer drenched a french fry in ketchup, then looked up at Red. "Well let's get up out of here. I'm getting full plus I wanna take a bubble bath at your house to let my body soak."

Red got up, went to the register to pay, and took his mother outside to head back to Bronxville.

* * *

Red dropped his mother off at his house so that she could relax. He knew she would be safe at his residence because no one knew where he lived. That was always something Razor told him: once you move out the hood, nobody from the hood should know where you rest at.

Red had to bust a few moves and knew Indiana would keep her company while he was gone. When he walked back in the door, he saw his mother and wifey laughing at some comedy movie on T.V.

Indiana noticed him instantly. "What's up baby? I missed you handsome! Come chill with me and mommy." She patted the cushion next to her on the big leather couch.

"Aight let me change up and put this away first." Red patted the duffle bag he had tucked under his armpit. He always tried to keep his street activities hidden from Indiana. The less that she knew, the better it was.

After Red stashed the money from his duffle, he jumped in the shower so he could change and relax with his family. When he got himself together he went down the stairs to see his mother rubbing on

Indiana's stomach. That visual was priceless in his mind: just seeing the two most important people in his life bonding together. That motivated him to the max.

"Okay I see y'all enjoying this quality time together." Red smiled and walked towards the couch.

"Yeah we are bonding what's wrong with that?" Indiana opened her arms waiting for a hug from the man she adored. Red squeezed her and continued to talk shit.

"Hold on, hold on," Jennifer interrupted. "Be quiet Red." She turned up the volume on the T.V.

"Police are still searching for suspects who shot up 183rd by Davidson Ave. Witnesses say there were two men: one Hispanic male about 5'8" and light-skinned, and one black male 6'0" and dark-skinned. If you have any information on the shooting please call 1-800-CRIMESTOPPERS. The commissioner believes this is just another part of the recent rise in violent crimes in the Bronx due to gang violence."

Red took the remote from Jennifer and switched the channel.

"Hey what are you doing? I was watching that!" Jennifer shook her head slowly from side to side.

Indiana got up from the couch, placing both of her hands on her hips in front of the T.V. "Look Red, I know what's going on. I know more than you think I do." A tear began to trickle down her cheek. "Baby, I want you to end this war you have going on! I don't want me, you, or our baby to get hurt. You know the streets don't have no limitations. They already tried to kidnap your mother and murder a few of your homies. Enough blood has spilled! When is enough enough?!"

Red knew this war was getting real intense and a lot of things were at stake. He wanted to put an end to the mayhem. Razor's words kept echoing in his head. ("If you cut off the head, the body will fall...")

How was he going to get at Mikey Fingaz? After Amber was thrown through the window of the restaurant, he closed that spot down. Red knew time was a tool for measurement and revealed all things. Good things happen to those who wait.

CHAPTER 16

Jennifer looked stunning in her black Fendi outfit. She was happy she finally was able to visit Razor at USP Big Sandy in Kentucky. This was the farthest she had traveled so far, but no distance would ever keep her away from her soulmate. She was reheating a coffee at the microwave in the visiting room when she glanced over, saw the door open, and Razor came walking out.

As soon as their eyes locked, a magnetic pull drew them together. Razor walked closer and smelled Jennifer's Chanel perfume that took his nostrils hostage. He immediately closed the distance between them, pulled her close, and grabbed her ass cheeks. He kissed her deeply, shoving his tongue far into her mouth. She used the moment to spit two balloons into his mouth.

"Alright!" they heard from behind them. "Break

up the kisses and sit down."

Razor broke up their lovey dovey session, glared back at the chubby C.O., and led Jennifer over to their seats. "Long time no see my elegant queen. I missed you so much! You have been on my mind every second of every day lately."

"I know baby. I've been meaning to come up here sooner but so much has been going on in the free world. You really need to talk with Red." Jennifer shifted anxiously in her seat and shook her head slowly from side to side. "He has a lot going on and whatever he's doing in the streets is beginning to affect me."

Razor could tell the situation was serious. "So tell me what's going on. You know I'll help y'all as much as I can from here." He sat back in his chair, folding his arms across his chest.

"Red is in a full-fledged war with the Russian mafia. Them Russians even went so far as trying to kidnap me the other night. I was so lucky to have made it out of that situation." Jennifer pointed out the scratch covering some of her cheek and her eye. She continued to explain what she knew, telling Razor the information came from Red's wifey who works for the N.Y.P.D.

Razor stared at the love of his life as his heart filled with rage. He was disappointed in himself for not being able to be there to protect his family. He felt as if he was powerless. If he were there, none of this would have happened.

"What's this MOB nigga's name? Do you know?" Razor asked.

Jennifer's answer confirmed the inside information he had gotten from his little homie Baby Boom. B.B. had been his eyes on the streets, watching Red for him ever since he'd been down. The two wrote back and forth, using the lingo Razor had created without the Feds all up in their business.

Her answers confirmed his Intel, but the abduction was new for him. Unfortunately, Razor didn't know if Red and his little homies were capable of winning this war. Things were happening rapidly, and they were in too deep to turn around now.

Razor's thoughts were interrupted by Jennifer. "Before I forget, Red's wifey Indiana asked you to call her urgently. I'll send you her number over email when I leave. She said to call from a safe line."

Jennifer grabbed some chips on the napkin off the table and relaxed a bit, knowing that she had passed on everything she needed to say.

CHAPTER 17

A few days later...

Red sat in his BMW 5-series crushing up some blueberry kush on a CD cover while B-Money sat next to him throwing cigar guts out the window. As he enjoyed the quiet, he thought about his birthday next month. While Red was thankful to reach as high as he got so far, he wasn't sure he'd make it to see that birthday. He had come a long way in such a short period of time but was afraid it was all about to crash down.

Red looked out the tinted window at the deserted block. Because of all the drama lately, no one wanted to be out on the streets anymore. This was definitely not why Red had worked as hard as he had: so that his neighborhood was all scared to even go outside. He sighed and took out his phone.

Red opened his Facebook app and signed in using a fake login. As he scrolled through the feed, he saw that Rolo was broadcasting on Facebook Live. With nothing else to do, he clicked on it.

The camera showed Rolo standing on the streets. "I can go anywhere I want! I go from borough to borough - can't nobody stop me. New York City is my playground!" Rolo spun the camera around, showing his viewers the scenery.

Red pulled his phone closer to his eyes, studying the background. Why did it look so familiar? Then he realized - that was the Step-In Lounge! Why was Rolo hanging out in his hood?

From Indiana's manilla folders, Red knew that Rolo was one of the main lieutenants for Mikey Fingaz. This was one of those times where luck and opportunity were intertwined.

Red put the car in drive and squealed onto the road. As the car jerked forward, B-Money spilled the blunt and weed flew everywhere.

"Damn Blood! You fucked up the L I was rollin."

Red didn't respond. He only had one thing on his mind, which was obvious by the way he drove recklessly through the streets. After speeding through all of the stop signs, red lights, and crosswalks, he pulled up in front of the Step-In Lounge.

"Yo Skrap — I'm looking for this Russian nigga I seen on Facebook Live out here." Red put down his window and scoped out the scene. The darkness was dense at 11 pm, and didn't aid his search. He double-parked in front of the spot, threw on his blinkers, and looked up. There was Rolo, staggering down the block with a white woman wrapped around him.

Rolo was definitely drunk. Red watched him cross the street, head down a cut block, and threw the car back in gear to follow. He watched as Rolo and the red-headed woman got into the car, shutting both doors and started up the engine.

Red stopped the car, hopped out, and grabbed his chrome .45 out of his pants with his right hand. He ran to the car as B-Money hopped out, following close behind with his .9 mil.

As Red reached the driver's side window, the woman saw him and the gun and immediately began laying on the horn. The butt of the .45 came crashing through the window, shattering glass everywhere. A high-pitched yelp came out as her survival tactics kicked in. She was stuck in the car, now boxed in by Red's BMW, and her companion was drunk. She looked out the other window and saw B-Money standing there, gun pointed at Rolo.

- BOOM - BOOM - BOOM -

Red shot the woman three times, splashing brain matter and blood all over the front seat, windshield, and dashboard. Her lifeless head fell on the steering wheel, sounding the horn again with her forehead; B-Money looked down both sides of the street, then let off a shot that shattered the passenger side window. Glass flew at Rolo's face and got in his eyes.

"Don't kill him Blood, we gonna take him somewhere first!" Red ran to the other side of the car, helping his man pull Rolo out of the window. He hit the pavement and felt blow after blow smack him from the butts of the two guns before falling unconscious.

"Ayo Blood, put this nigga in my trunk. Help me out." Red dragged Rolo's body towards his Beamer as B-Money clicked the button to open the trunk. Both of them picked up the body and dumped it head-first in the car, then closed it tight.

They started the car, drove to the highway, and headed to Bronxville. Rolo's unconscious body bounced around in the trunk, bleeding from two huge gashes in the face from the pistol-whipping. After about 20 minutes, they arrived to a vacant house on the block.

B-Money looked puzzled. "Homie where the fuck we at?"

"Just chill Blood, we about to have a little fun."

Red pulled in the driveway and kept going all the way to the backyard fence. The houses were far enough apart from each-other that it was pitch black in the backyard. Red cut the engine, drew his gun, and got out.

Red turned to B-Money. "Yo Blood, get that flashlight out the glove compartment for me real quick. When I pop the trunk we gonna grab him and drag him to the shed back there."

B-Money grabbed the flashlight and his gun, pointing them at the shed before walking over to the trunk.

Red popped the trunk open as B-Money trained his gun at Rolo. They both heard grunting and moaning as Rolo held his head with one hand. Blood covered his entire face.

B-Money cocked his gun back and started swinging it wildly. He slammed it a few times at Rolo, hitting him on the head on the final blow. Rolo dropped and went limp.

Red and B-Money dragged the body through the backyard into a little green shed. Red opened the lock, threw open the door, then pulled the string on the ceiling which illuminated the inside. Rakes, shovels, ropes, and wood littered the floor. A chair stood in the center of the room and a menacing chainsaw sat in the corner.

"Yo let's sit this nigga in the chair and tie him up before he regains consciousness."

They tied Rolo to the chair, making sure his arms and legs were knotted good. B-Money began slapping him with one hand in the face a few times.

It only took six slaps for Rolo to wake up.

As Rolo opened his eyes, he saw he was in a toolshed tied to a chair. Even with all that, he stayed surprisingly calm and looked back and forth from Red to B-Money.

Red stared right back at him, showing no fear. "Look. Fuck all the bullshit. Where can I find your boss at?"

"My man, I could never give up my boss. That would compromise my morals and principles." Rolo licked the blood from his busted lip. "Do what you have to do with me. I'll die with pride."

"I'm just gonna ask you this one question and then I'll be satisfied. Did you try and kidnap my mother?"

Rolo started laughing hysterically. "You talking about the Spanish woman with that big ole ass."

Red growled, snatched his gun, and shot Rolo in the forehead. As blood oozed out on the wood floor, Red walked to the corner, grabbed the chainsaw, and turned it on.

"Yo bro pull his head back so I can cut it off." Red wasn't messing around. B-Money held his head while Red chiseled three cuts across the neck, severing the head from the body.

Red picked up Rolo's head by its hair as blood dripped on the floor.

"I always wanted to try some gruesome shit! Just shooting people gets boring after a while.

Everybody ain't doing no shit like this though."

B-Money backed up a step, staring surprised at Red. He just witnessed Red take things to a whole new level. He picked up a black backpack from the floor and handed it to Red, helping, him stuff the head inside before zipping it up.

Red pulled the string, cutting the lights to the shed. "Come on bro, I got somewhere to take this head to. I'll bury his body in the backyard later on it's good for right now.

They got in the BMW and jumped on the highway headed towards Mikey Fingaz' gambling spot. That was where this whole beef had started, and that's where Red planned to end it. As he signaled I to get off on the next exit, they heard a police siren and saw lights directly behind them.

"Oh shit big bro, we going down! It's all over!" B-Money shouted, shaking his head nervously from side to side.

"Chill out, it might not be nothing." Red slowed down and began to pull off the road. "But once they say anything about searching the vehicle or 'step out of the car' we gotta let them have it. Get ready to bust your hammer!"

Just as he pulled onto the shoulder, the police car zoomed past them.

Red's heartbeat was beating fast - he was nervous as hell. Shit, he had a person's head in a backpack right behind him on the back seat.

"Damn that was a close one!" Red calmed down and started to laugh. "Yo homie you was shook nigga talking about we going down, it's over, blah blah blah. It sounded like you were about to cry next. There's tissues in the glove compartment."

Red pulled back onto the highway, got off at the next exit, and headed to the gambling spot. As they pulled up, they noticed a few people lingering, out front. Most of them were smoking cigarettes or on their phones. Red scanned the crowd to look for Mikey Fingaz, but didn't spot him.

Red took another lap around the block, telling B-Money to throw Rolo's head out the window at the crowd.

B-Money tossed the head right into the crowd, and several people started to scream. Red peeled off in the car so that no one could get a licence plate number off him.

B-Money screamed "Fuck Russians!" out the window as they sped off. Red knew that in war you had to make bold moves to win the battles.

"Hello is this Indiana?" Razor paced back and forth in his cell anxiously.

"Yeah," Indiana replied. "This must be Razor, right? Jennifer said she gave you my number. I'm elated that you reached out." She continued to stir her rice in a pot in the kitchen.

"This line is secure, so you can let me know in depth what's going on. From what Jennifer told me it's very important that you have my assistance. I want to let you know that you are my family now, so anything in my power I will make happen." Razor paused to let his words sink in, then continued. "By the way, how is my grandbaby doing in your stomach?"

Indiana took a deep breath. "Well I'm pretty sure you know there is a full fledged war between the Russian mob and the Neighborhood Gangstas.

I want it to end. So many people have already died and gotten hurt. I don't want anything bad to happen to Red, me, or the baby. I especially don't want Red going to prison for the rest of his life."

"Yeah, I've heard some things through the grapevine about all this. So what's this Russian dude's name? And where's he located?" Razor walked over to his desk and grabbed a pen to write down some details. As he did this, he glanced to the door to make sure two of his homies were still watching out for the police.

"The head Russian is Michael Kujovich but they call him Mikey Fingaz. And if you have something to write with, I'll give you his information."

Indiana read off his information from a folder in the kitchen as Razor wrote it all down. As he wrote, he got a crazy feeling of deja vu – like he had heard the name before but just couldn't remember where.

"Aight. I got all the details scribbled down. I'm

gonna see what I can do to alleviate the problem. I'll reach out to a few of my people out in Cali to see what's up. Now I got your number so I'll keep you updated too. Don't be a stranger either. And don't get too fat or Red gonna leave your ass!"

"Alright Razor keep me posted on any details. And Red is stuck with me for life now - whether I'm skinny, tall, fat, or small. Best get that right!"

Razor heard someone shout "Whoop!" behind him. "Yo I gotta go - the C.O. is coming." Razor ended the call and stashed the phone in a spot behind the toilet. Just as he got it put away, the C.O. knocked on the door and opened it.

"Terrell Washington? You have to go to medical immediately." The skinny, white officer took a look around, closed the door, and walked back to the office.

* * *

Red's BMW 5 Series was parked outside Angel's strip club, the LED lights illuminated the ground in alternating shades of red. Red smoked a blunt of purple haze as he sat in the front seat listening to Big Deal's new hit single "Been On." He was grateful to finally see the day of his birthday, especially after all of the drama with the Russians the past few months. He took another deep pull from the blunt, looked down the block, and waited for more of his homies to pull up.

There was already a gang of them standing in front of Angel's, but Red wanted to wait for   B-Money to pull up before the party really got started.

Lately Red and Bandz had been growing farther apart from each other. B-Money had become his right-hand man for the past month or so. Bandz may have been a bit distant, but he was still invited to his birthday party.

As Red inhaled another long drag from the haze, his mind drifted back to memories from the past year: everything from how he met the love of his life to how serious the beef had gotten.

Red was deep in thought when all of a sudden a knock on the window startled him. He looked up and saw B-Money and Apple standing there. Red pressed the button to let the window down, and a thick cloud of smoke smacked B-Money in the face.

"Damn Blood! You getting smacked in here huh?" B-Money sniffed the air like a dog smelling out table scraps. "What kind of bud is that?"

Red looked behind B-Money and saw Apple standing with her hands on her hips. She glanced at him, then over at the club, impatiently.

Red followed her eyes and saw the advertising for his birthday bash everywhere. He didn't want all the attention because of the war between him and the Russians, but his homies couldn't resist. There were posters, signs, and shout-outs on Power 105 and Hot 97. B-Money definitely knew how to do a party right.

Red left his BMW with half a blunt hanging from his lips as he scanned inside the parked cars across the street. He had been extra cautious ever since the Russians had been coming on his turf. They proved to be as unpredictable as they were vicious and Red wasn't taking any chances.

Luckily the coast was clear, so he tucked two chrome 9 millimeters into his Gucci belt, threw on his hoodie, and shut the car door behind him. "Su-Whoopppp!" was all Red heard as he walked towards the entrance to Angel's. So many familiar faces were scattered amongst the crowd. In total, there were over 150 Neighborhood Gangstas that had showed up for the birthday bash. Plus, the line to get in was wrapped around the block. Red saw gorgeous women wearing all kinds of tight clothing and a few celebrities in the line as well.

"What's good Blood?" Flex threw up the neighborhood handshake with Red and embraced him.

Red saw the security jacket. Flex was wearing. "You work at this spot now?"

"Yeah. I had to find another job after the police raided Show Palace. One thing about it - the grind don't stop!"

"Ayo Red - your boo crossing the street coming

this way!" Apple shouted loud enough for the first hundred people in line to hear her. As she put on some more glossy, pink lipstick, everybody looked across the street to see Bandz and Roses coming their way.

'Thank God I told Indiana to stay at home,' Red thought. 'If not, things might have spiraled out of control.' At first, she wasn't trying to hear that until Red reminded her she was pregnant. He didn't want anything to happen to her or the baby with them Russians around.

Roses strutted across the street like she was on America's Top Model.

She looked like she was straight off the runway too - wearing the latest all-red catsuit by Dolce & Gabanna. Everyone waiting for the club had eyes on her, even Red.

Roses looked at Red and held his eyes hostage longer than usual. She didn't break eye contact until Bandz pulled her close to him and whispered something in her ear. Secretly Red missed Roses because of their long history together. They had so many memories that he would never truly forget. Red would always have a soft spot for Roses but would never admit it to anyone.

"Happy birthday Blood!" Roses walked up and kissed Red on the cheek. "I'm ready to turn up - I need a good time!"

Red hugged her and couldn't help but look her

tight body up and down as she kissed his cheek. Damn she was fine as hell.

B-Money's tap on his shoulder got him out of his thoughts. "You ready to go inside Red?"

Red nodded and walked down the line towards Flex at the front. As he walked he got birthday wishes from everybody around. Even 50 Cent and Straight Stuntin model Skittles were there and gave dap.

Flex pulled out a clipboard as Red walked up. "Come on inside Red. Who is everybody going in with you?"

"Ayo Blood. I gotta bring my ladies in with me." Red pointed at the two bulges under his hoodie.

Flex's grin disappeared and he looked serious. "Aight. Just you though, nobody else, bro. Please." Flex ushered Red to the lobby with him so he could pass them off. After that, Red and his whole team came through the metal detector and cleared the searches.

As soon as they got into the strip club, Red's eyes were assaulted with beautiful women. He looked around and saw two in particular that interested him - two twins that were working the floor. They were about 5'6", cinnamon complexion, with short black hair and tattoos from the neck down. They were wearing skin-tight outfits that left little of their amazing bodies to the imagination. Each one of them smiled at Red, and one of them took a handful of her breast, sticking out her tongue at Red.

Red led his team to the V.I.P. section, where they had reserved all the tables. He had to push his way through the crowd - the club was packed already! Between the exotic women running around half-naked and different types of smoke filling the air, Red knew it was gonna be a lit night.

On the way to the V.I.P. section, Flex made his way through the crowd and passed off Red's two 9 millimeters back discretely. Red nodded at him and continued to walk through the crowd.

The bouncer let Red through to the V.I.P. section along with his entire entourage. After they were all inside, the twin that had grabbed her titty came up to Red and licked her lips.

"What kind of bottles you want, handsome? And how many?"

Red stopped for a second, captivated by her beauty. "I - uh - want five bottles of Henny and five bottles of Patron." He went into his jeans pocket to retrieve some money to pay for the bottles.

B-Money looked over and slapped Red's hand away. "Ayo Blood, you ain't gotta pay for anything bro. It's already paid for ya dig?" He gave Red a sly grin, noticing the way he was looking at the twin.

Just then, "Drip too Hard" by Lil Baby came blaring out the speakers and Red started to bob his head up and down to the beat. DJ Self kept shouting out Red in between his mixes. Red truly felt like a celebrity outside of his hood tonight.

Red decided it would be the perfect time to sit back and relax. He cracked a dutch and walked over to one of the red velvet couches that lined the V.I.P. section. Just as he put his feet up, ten beautiful women walked in a line straight towards him. Each one held a huge bottle with sparklers coming out of the top. At the head of the pack was the twin that had caught Red's attention at the beginning of the night. After placing her bottle on his table, she sat down right next to Red, her gorgeous legs touching his.

Red leaned close to her and spoke in her ear so he could be heard over the booming bass. "So what is your name? And why you on my line like this? Somebody sent you my way? Because one thing I do know the power of pussy is a muthafucka!" He leaned forward to dump the insides of the dutch into a small garbage can.

"My name is Cindy but everybody calls me CeCe for short." She pointed to her twin, who was walking over towards the table just then. "And my twin's name is Mindy. The reason why I'm on you like this is because you are truly attractive and I want to see what's up with the birthday boy." CeCe punctuated these last few words with a wink as she grabbed a handful of Red's crotch. Just then, Mindy sat down on the opposite side of Red.

Roses watched all of this transpire - the hand

gestures, the flirting, and the grabbing between Red and the twin sisters. She wasn't feeling none of that right there, plus the liquor had her thinking all kinds of thoughts.

At the end of the day, Red was her first love. She would always have love for him no matter what.

"Ayo Bandz," Red said, "tell Apple to bring me that half ounce of kush so I could smoke. Because after I smoke this blunt I ain't got no more - good looking out."

Bandz turned to Red and stared blankly. "I ain't doing shit blood! You get your ass up and do it yourself - you ain't got no slaves over here my nigga!"

Red got up off the couch and slowly walked towards Bandz, until the two of them were standing toe-to-toe and face-to-face. Both of them had on a cold stare.

"Yo Red, after all this shit clears up with these punk-ass Russians I'm thinking about starting my own branch." Bandz spoke his piece firmly as he surveyed the crowd that started to form.

Red blinked and let aggression seep into his voice. "Nigga who the fuck gonna follow you? This is my shit!"

"Nah," Bandz said, shaking his head. "That's where you got it fucked up. It's supposed to be our shit."

"You were dead pussy when I first met you! I

made you into who you are - never forget that son!" Red cocked back his right fist and connected with Bandz' jawline, knocking him to the floor instantly. B-Money ran to Red's side and grabbed his shoulder. "Hold up, hold up - y'all niggas is buggin right now! We brothers!" He led Red back towards the exit of the V.I.P. section, trying to difuse the situation. He could see that the liquor had Red going. At the same time Roses stood in the background shaking her head with a smile plastered across her face.

Just as B-Money was calming down one situation, another fight broke out by the bar between two broads. Flex and the rest of the security team came running to the scene to break it up.

Red let B-Money lead him back to the couch, where he took a seat and scanned the room, finding Apple. He gave her the keys to his Beamer and asked her to grab some bud out of the stash.

The other homies decided to remove Bandz from the party to eliminate the possibility of more tension between him and Red. No one wanted a second altercation the night of Red's birthday. Roses gave Bandz a kiss, but stayed at the club. She could always catch an Uber or something to get home later.

Red lit up another blunt and the twins both started to give him a lap dance at the same time.

He threw up singles and tried to handle both of them. They had his hormones sky-high as they were both twerking. Just as Red was about to take another swig out of his Patron bottle, he heard a loud explosion and all of the front windows of the club shattered.

Both twins immediately cuddled up into Red's arms as people ran around frantically trying to dodge for cover. The music stopped playing and the sound of tires screeching flooded the club.

Red's first thought was about Apple. He had just sent her outside minutes ago to grab some bud. He shot up from the couch and took off towards the exit. When he made it outside, he saw his Beamer burnt to a crisp, glass scattered all over the sidewalk and surrounding street. The explosion must have been huge: several other cars were on fire as well as a local store. Apple was nowhere in sight.

As he walked closer to his car, Red could think of nothing but the Russians He could see two legs sticking out from behind the back tire, and immediately thought the worst. Walking over, he saw Apple's body, charred and bleeding out on the pavement. A tear trickled down his face as it all hit him. Red knew it was his fault - if he hadn't told her to get the bud she would still be alive!

Apple was like his little sister. He had grown up with her and Roses. They were best friends too!

Red got down on one knee next to Apple's body and a bunch of people came out of the club to see what had happened. B-Money, Roses, and a few other Neighborhood homies were in the crowd.

Roses spotted Red kneeling down next to his car and ran over to him. Her heart skipped a beat when she saw that it was Apple's lifeless body sprawled across the street.

Red looked back over his shoulder at Roses and embraced her as she began to cry hysterically. He heard sirens getting closer and began fuming at all of the thoughts in his head.

CeCe grabbed Red by the elbow. "It's gonna be alright pa. Come on - let's walk to your car so you can head home."

Red shook his head side-to-side in disbelief. "My car was the one that got blown up. I'm gonna have to get one of my homies to take me home." By now, his high had evaporated and he was instantly sober.

CeCe stared into Red's eyes. "Well me and my sister can drop you off anywhe you need us to. I feel so bad for you and I wanna help any way I possibly can."

Just then, a NYPD car and ambulance arrived on the scene. Red hung around to see what type of interrogation the police had in store. He didn't want to be dragged along to the police station or have to answer any questions.

Luckily, all of the questions were targeted at Roses, since she was draped across Apple's body, crying hysterically.

CeCe took Red's hand inside hers and walked him towards her white Nissan Maxima. Her sister Mindy followed in pursuit.

"Yo Blood where you headed?" B-Money yelled after him.

Red turned, looked back across the street at B-Money, and waited for him to catch up. "I'm about to dip and head back to the crib, homie. This shit with Apple messed up my whole mood and my night ya dig? Just make sure Roses gets home safe and sound." Red turned back to continue walking with the twins. "Hit, me up when you two make it home."

They threw up the Neighborhood handshake and Red climbed in the back seat of the Maxima. CeCe climbed in next to him while her sister Mindy started up the car. They had already told the owner that they were leaving for the night so they didn't have to come back to work.

"So where you want us to drop you off?" Mindy asked as she looked at Red through the rearview mirror.

"You can take me to 548 Leland Avenue in the Bronx. I'll be good there. I really appreciate y'all holding me down without even knowing me at all. That's real shit though." He tied a red du-rag around his head and leaned back in the seat.

CeCe instantly started to touch up Red's thigh. She was so attracted to Red ever since she first laid eyes on him.

So many thoughts were running through Red's mind. He had lost a lot of people close to him - so many he started to get numb to the pain. One more person had just died that meant a lot to him - someone he had known since a little kid. Red's thoughts got interrupted as CeCe began to unbuckle his belt and jeans. Red didn't say anything - he just went with the flow.

Red had never cheated on Indiana before, so it felt a little weird at first. He was about to stop CeCe, but then felt her warm mouth devour his manhood. With every suck and slurp he got more in the mood. Feelings of depression and hurt got sent to the back of his mind while pleasure and excitement came.

Red wrapped a handful of her hair around his fist as CeCe's head bops got more intense by the second. The sensation was so amazing that Red leaned his head back and enjoyed CeCe's professional head game.

"Girl go faster!" Mindy said to her sister. "Stop playing with him!" She watched eagerly from the rearview mirror.

Mindy's juices started flowing between her legs as she heard CeCe's slurps begin to overpower the radio in the car. Mindy kept her right hand on the steering wheel but moved her left hand down to play with her pussy. Red's eyes popped open as he heard Mindy moan from the front seat.

"Pull over to the closest spot you see cause it's about to get real," CeCe said as she took Red's dick out of her mouth briefly. "Let's give the birthday boy a present he will never forget!"

CHAPTER 18

Instead of driving back to Red's crib Mindy pulled up to the curb of the Four Seasons Hotel in Manhattan. Red threw the keys at the attendant, flashed his black card at the desk, and led the two ladies up to a penthouse suite at the top of one of the most expensive buildings in the city.

On the elevator ride up, Red knew that he was all in. This was gonna be a birthday that he would never forget.

Once they got inside the room, it became a scene out of a Buttman magazine. CeCe opened the door to the bedroom, then pushed Red on the bed. She jumped on top of him and started to tongue kiss him passionately. As they kissed, CeCe stripped off his clothes as Red's hands explored her curvaceous body.

While Red and CeCe had their lips locked, Mindy took off all of her clothes beside the bed and admired the view of the city.

"Ayo Mindy!" Red's words brought her back to the hotel room. "You come here on the bed and lay down on your back. CeCe start eating your sister's pussy bent over doggy-style position." Red slowly stroked his erection and eagerly awaited his commands to play out before his eyes.

Mindy positioned herself and CeCe began flicking her tongue across her sister's clit. Red came up behind her and pushed his manhood inside her tight wet vagina. A moan escaped her mouth as his penis filled her perfectly. Red started pumping CeCe from the back as he smacked her ass cheeks with an open palm. CeCe was so turned on that she couldn't even concentrate on eating out her sister.

Mindy inserted her index and middle fingers inside her pussy as she watched Red slide in and out of her sister. CeCe's facial expressions drove her sister wild. Mindy started to increase the pace that she fingered herself: faster and faster.

"Uhh... Ohh... Uhh!" CeCe moaned. "Damn this shit feels so good - go faster, Red!" She bit her bottom lip seductively and stared him in the face.

Red grabbed her love handles and started thrusting even faster. All you could hear was the sound of moaning and skin clapping. Just as Red pulled his dick out of CeCe to change positions, Mindy leaned over and started sucking the pussy juices off Red's pulsating rod.

Mindy's head game was on another level and the suction she was giving had Red ready to bust a nut already. But he was trying to enjoy this threesome. It was his first one ever, so he wanted to take advantage of the situation at hand. Soon enough CeCe came to join the fun and both women exchanged saliva over his manhood.

Red put one hand behind each of their heads and leaned back, embracing pure ecstasy.

"Let me ride that dick!" Mindy licked her lips seductively at Red and pushed him back on the bed. She climbed on top of him and straddled him like a cowgirl. "Ooh... Oooh... Uhh... Ahh..." Her screams got louder and louder as she bounced up and down on Red's manhood. He grabbed at her 36 D's as they jiggled around.

Red decided to take control, grabbing Mindy's love handles firmly and began thrusting in and out at a quicker pace. The two locked eyes as the sounds of sex got louder and louder. It was obvious that both Mindy and Red were really getting into it.

CeCe saw the action, and started to get a bit jealous. She really wanted Red all for herself.

"Oh my God I'm about to cum!" Mindy's eyes rolled into the back of her head as she started to gush.

Red didn't want to nut because he wanted to bust CeCe for real this time. Once Mindy nutted, he slid out of her and told CeCe to suck up her sister's juices. CeCe crawled over to him and went right to work - putting her tongue ring into action.

Red enjoyed a few moments of her mouth, but then laid her down in missionary position and put both her legs behind her head. Once he slid inside, he started stroking very fast in and out of her tight, wet pussy. Red started to suck on her right titty as he hit her long-dick style. After a few more strokes he couldn't last, and erupted inside CeCe.

CeCe wrapped her legs around his waist so she could receive every drop of his semen. The sensation of releasing his sperm made Red not even think twice about what she was doing. Usually he would have strapped up, but between his hormones and the situation at hand he slipped up. Hopefully it wouldn't cost him in the long run. After busting his nut, he laid down next to both women.

Red looked left and right at the beautiful twins laying down next to him. He was on cloud nine after the episode that had just taken place. What a birthday present this was: two exotic twins with him for a night in the hotel room.

He thought to himself that this was a memory he would never forget.

CHAPTER 19

"Yo Blood!" Razor's voice could be heard all the way from the top tier throughout the entire unit. "Tell the fool DL to come up here real quick."

Razor walked back inside the cell and grinned. D-Mack, Kapone, Tyke, and the newest blood on the unit, Fury, were all lounging around passing a couple of bottles filled with white lightning. Everyone was laughing and joking around until Ryder and DL came inside the cell.

By this time, it had been about five months already since DL had owed Diablo a few thousand dollars. Razor ended up getting the Blood car for the compound after his property got there. And one thing most cars don't tolerate is owing debts. Razor refused to just sweep this situation under the rug.

"Close that door Blood, you don't see me rollin

up this sticky icky?" Tyke smirked as he looked up at Ryder.

DL took a seat on the bottom bunk next to Fury and looked around at all the white lightning.

"So DL what's up Damu?" Razor grabbed a bottle and extended it out to DL. "You ain't trying to drink none of this gas right here?"

DL grabbed the bottle and took a squirt of the prison liquor. At the same time, Fury acted like he was getting up, but instead spun around in one swift motion with a shank drawn in his right hand.

Kapone drew his metal knife from his waistband and charged DL. Fury was already on him stabbing him in the face and upper torso. DL fruitlessly tried to block the blows coming from all directions.

"Ahh Blood chill out! Please stop homie!" DL screamed at the top of his lungs. He knew he needed to get someone's attention as people walked by.

What DL didn't know was that Razor had already spoken with Diablo. He had all of the Mexicans yelling loudly as they played dominos, which caused the entire unit to be louder than usual.

One thing about the Feds - when someone was getting a move brought to them, everybody else knew except the person that the harm was coming to.

All of the Blood homies were putting in work now. DL tried to make a run for the cell door but

Razor put him in a dope fean before he could make a successful escape. He continued to scream to no avail.

There was blood splattered all over the cell: from the bed sheets to the ceiling. DL had lost so much blood that he fell in and out of consciousness. The move the homies had brought caught DL by surprise. It was completely unexpected.

DL had a moment of clarity, broke out of Razor's grip, and rushed at Tyke swinging wildly. This time the assault got out to the tier.

Razor saw DL bust out of the cell and started yelling. "Kapone and Ryder! Finish that nigga! You know they about to hit the deuces any minute!"

DL couldn't see anything because of the blood covering both of his eyes. He never saw Ryder come out of the cell on a mission. He never saw Ryder plunge his shank on the top of his head, where it got stuck. All he felt was the pain then dropped to the floor instantly from the blow.

Kapone and Tyke started to kick DL in his head as hard as they could. By now, the entire unit watched as the attack continued. After a few more kicks, they grabbed DL by his ankles and wrists. Walking towards the stairs, they threw him down head-first directly in front of the C.O. bubble.

The C.O. jumped up from his chair at the noise and noticed DL sprawled across the floor lifeless, blood covering the entire upper half of his body. The

C.O. pressed his body alarm, setting into motion a call for assistance.

Kapone, Tyke, and Ryder dipped off into a Crip homie Tiny Milk's cell to drop off the knives so he could stash them.

Diablo sat at the domino table, in full view of the entire incident. It had gone down exactly as expected. Diablo not only had a lot of faith in Razor, but also respect for how he moved.

Within a few minutes, the entire unit was filled with C.O.s shouting, carrying cans of mace and guns filled with rubber bullets.

"Everybody lock in your cells right now! Hurry up!" The tall, skinny captain hid behind the rest of the C.O.s as he attempted to direct traffic.

Everyone slowly walked to their cells, complying with the police's demands. Razor and Kapone looked out the door from their cell as they all surrounded DL. Minutes passed by, and still his body lay there motionless. Razor thought he had died, but from the way the medics treated him, it appeared he was just knocked out unconscious.

After minutes had passed, DL came to and shook his head a bit. He was helped to a stretcher, where he shouted loud enough for the entire unit to hear. "Y'all busta niggas know what it is!"

Razor looked on and saw that the knife Ryder had stuck in his head was still pointing out at a morbid angle. He turned back to Kapone with a smirk on his face, shaking his head from side to side. "I can't lie blood, the homies had worked him good. We got some official homies on this block right here."

After the C.O. came around to lock all of the cell doors, Razor began the cleanup process. He took off his shirt, tore it into small shredded pieces, and slowly flushed them down the toilet one by one. There were small specks of blood all over his shirt: he needed to destroy all of the evidence before they called him in for questions.

Just as he finished the cleanup and put on his R-10 headphones to zone out for a nap, a C.O. came to his door.

"Hey both of y'all cuff up. Come on!" the C.O. shouted through the tiny food slot in the door. "The captain would like to speak to both of y'all." The chubby, bald C.O. was flanked by two other officers as they waited for wrists to come through the slot and put on the handcuffs.

The five of them walked out of the unit, through the prison, and down a long corridor headed to the captain's office. Razor and Kapone walked through the door and saw a bunch of staff members they had never even seen before.

"Mr. Washington, I'm well aware that you are the shot caller to the Blood car on my compound," Investigator Cornwell said as he munched on a donut. Cornwell worked for Special Investigative Services (S.I.S.) at the prison, and it was his job to know everything that happened on the compound. "And I would like to know a few things before I send you to the SHU."

Razor flinched. He had spent time in the Special Housing Unit before, and would do it again if he had to, but being in isolation for months - and sometimes years - while the police did an investigation on him was not his idea of doing good time.

Before Razor could reply, Kapone spoke up. "Look. I punished the dude. Mr. Washington didn't even know what was going on." Kapone gestured towards Razor as he spoke, maintaining eye contact with S.I.S.

"He didn't sanction anything. So if you gonna take someone to the box, take me not both of us." Kapone looked around the room at each of the high-ranking prison guards.

Razor stood next to Kapone, shocked and dumbfounded. He was always one to take the pressure and roll with the punches. He was all set to go to the box, and then Kapone went and said that to them people. That was a true nigga right there.

Kapone took the weight for two reasons: 1. He already had four life sentences, so he didn't really care about going to the box. Prison was already his residence. 2. He didn't want Razor to get written up and go to the SHU. Razor had just finished the S.M.U. program, and was all set to spend the rest of his time outside the hole. He didn't want to see his homie go right back into the box like this.

The lieutenant looked at the captain and shrugged his shoulders. "Okay then, take the cuffs off Washington and take Smith to segregation. I guess our investigation came to a halt." He waited for his officers to remove the cuffs and then addressed Razor directly. "Mr. Washington, you lucked out today thanks to one of your comrades. I will be watching you very closely from here on out. Go back to your unit now. Thank you for your time."

Razor watched and waited as the lieutenant's pale white face slowly got very red.

CHAPTER 20

"Come in here baby!" Bandz yelled from the living room couch. "I need some head after watching this movie. Halle Berry getting a nigga hype peeling out her clothes - real talk." He rubbed his crotch impatiently as Roses folded clothes in the bedroom.

Roses and Bandz had been real attached lately. They had gotten so serious that Roses was staying overnight at his apartment at least five nights a week. In addition, Roses had just revealed to Bandz that her pregnancy test had come back positive last week. She didn't plan to get pregnant, but she did want to just feel loved.

Roses had a lot on her mind lately. She was still undecided if she wanted to keep the baby. Her plan was always to settle down with Red eventually. He was her first love, and that was still where her heart was at.

Roses snapped out of her thoughts and made her way to the living room, where Bandz was sprawled out on the couch. "Now what did you just fix your mouth to tell me?" Roses stood calmly in front of the T.V. with her black robe opened wide, exposing all her goodies.

Lust was in Bandz' eyes as he stared at this woman, mesmerized by her sex appeal. "I said give me some slow neck. Halle Berry got me going after this movie I just watched." Bandz licked his lips slowly as he waited for Roses to respond.

"Nigga who you talking to like that? I ain't none of these thot bitches that work on demand! Call Halle Berry to lick your dick since she was the one you were fantasizing about!" Roses was furious.

Bandz started to laugh. "Come on, bitch. Stop fronting and let me nut in your mouth! You need some protein anyway."

"Yo you talking wild disrespectful. It's aight to say what you want to me, but you ain't have that energy when you were talking to Red you clown-ass nigga!"

Roses words cut Bandz deep. It hurt his ego because deep down he knew Roses still had feelings for Red. He knew that he was incomparable to Red in stature, swag, intelligence, and as a man.

One thing about the truth: it don't need a kickstand to stand on. Once Roses stormed out of the living room, her words were like tattoos on the walls of Bandz' cranium. Hearing something like that from your woman would take its toll on any man - especially if it was true. Lately, Roses had been emotionally off-balance and her verbal interactions had reached the pinnacle of disrespect. Between her being pregnant and her best friend Apple getting killed, she didn't know how to feel.

When it comes down to it, there are only three reasons why people join gangs. Because they believe in the cause that the gang was created for, for protection, or for acceptance. When it's the third reason, they substitute the love they're missing from their own families for that of the gang.

'Well,' Roses thought, 'I guess either you choose the game or the game chooses you...'

CHAPTER 21

It had been two weeks at USP Big Sandy since Razor spoke with Indiana. He had heard all about the situation between the Neighborhood Gangstas and the Russian mob. As he sat in the unit, so many different scenarios played through his mind.

One thing Razor had learned through the years was that you can't solve problems by using the same kind of thinking you used when you first created the problem. That was a truth he embedded deep with Red a long time ago. Part of Razor's thoughts drifted to the deep disappointment he felt with Red, that he wasn't using those lessons.

Even though he was in the pen, Razor knew it was going to be on him to step up and get rid of the drama between his set and the Russians. As he thought, he heard a ten-minute recreation move over the loudspeaker of his unit.

Razor put on his Air Force Ones and Gucci sunglasses and walked outside. It was a hot July summer day, which meant that everyone was headed outside. The corridor was packed with inmates waiting to clear the metal detector.

"Yo Razor!" Diablo said. "Hold up my man, I want to spin the yard with you." Diablo walked past two Surenos and stood in line next to Razor. The two embraced briefly, then walked through the metal detector.

Diablo and Razor walked out towards the A yard as a bunch of people yelled salutes through the fences of the B and C yards. Within the Feds, both were known as reputable gang members and were always extended the utmost respect.

"Come on," Diablo gestured. "Let's go sit up by the bench right there. He pointed towards a vacant bench in the far right corner of A yard. About ten Surenos stood nearby as security for Diablo since he was the only Black Hand (Mexican Mafia) on the entire compound.

Normally the gang was right by his side, no matter where he went. However, when Diablo was with Razor, they stood back a respectful distance at Diablo's order.

One thing was for sure: every Sureno carried a knife on them at all times while they watched from a distance.

Diablo sat down, then gestured next to him on the bench for Razor to do the same. "What's up my man? You've been distant these past two weeks. What seems to be the issue? I consider you one of my comrades despite the gang affiliations. If I can help you in any way possible I will do just that."

"It's nothing personal against you. I just been dealing with this problem and trying to find the best solution. Sometimes making things happen from in here can take a long time to handle." Razor slowly shook his head in disappointment.

The conversation made Razor think back on his intel gathering. He had reached out to a few of his homies in California to acquire some information on Mikey Fingaz. Razor was frustrated by how slow the investigation was going. He still had no idea who he wanted to entrust with the mission at hand. There weren't too many other people he knew that had the credentials to succeed.

Diablo patiently waited, watching Razor's mind at work. "So let me know what's going on homes? A closed mouth never gets fed."

"Well," Razor said with a clenched jaw, "my set has been going to war lately. My stepson has been out in them streets acting a damn fool and got a lot of innocent people caught up in the crossfire." The entire time he kept his eyes on the handball courts.

"Who have y'all been going to war with?"

"This guy named Mikey Fingaz. The name

sounds so familiar but I can't put a face on him. I tried to google him from the phone, but nothing pops up except some shit about his son dying on Rikers Island!" Razor pounded the side of the bench with his fist in anger, as he glanced over at Diablo. He realized that Diablo's entire facial expression changed as soon as he mentioned the name Mikey Fingaz.

"Mikey Fingaz?!? That rat-bastard Russian mob muthafucka from California? I tried to get him killed before, but the mission wasn't complete. They did a sloppy job. This guy was the one who killed my brother back on the turf. I have been wanting revenge for a while now. You got a landline on him?" Diablo's voice dripped with anticipation.

"Yeah - I ain't know any of that right there." Razor started to sound more enthusiastic already. "We got a common enemy right now. My stepson's wifey is a police officer and she gave me a bunch of information about him including his place of residence. He lives in Staten Island in New York City."

Diablo's face grew serious. "Mira. My nephews are from Mexico. They are part of the notorious Sinaloa cartel. And I have a few good people from Chihuahua. They control the entire middle of Mexico. They were ex-military police and they take care of all the high-profile killings."

Diablo paused and looked Razor dead in the

eyes. "It's obvious your stepson doesn't have the qualifications to handle this or your opposition would have been history already. I will handle this for you if you give me the word. It's personal for me as well. I would just like to make sure it's done right with no mistakes. I don't want him to get away again." He looked down at his lap. "Let me ask you this question right here Razor - if your stepson missed the shot, would you have him killed?"

"No I wouldn't. Everybody makes mistakes all the time," Razor replied, saying exactly the words Diablo knew he would say.

"That's the difference right there homeboy! If they miss, they die. These men are experts. The last time I sent some gang bangers with heart to kill and they messed up. This time I'm sending my men who I know won't fail."

Razor nodded his head as Diablo's words marinated in his head. He trusted Diablo and wouldn't mind the favor. In the gang world when obstacles arise, sometimes someone you least expect will help get the job done. One hand washes the other and they both wash the face. At the end of the day, the outcome is a win.

Razor and Diablo continued their conversation until they called a yard recall.

CHAPTER 22

Weeks later...

It was a scorching hot August day. The sun was beaming like never before. The hood was packed with kids running in the street. As they ran in and out of the water from fire hydrants, damn-near naked women watched from the stoops. A lot of the Neighborhood Gangstas were rolling up weed in the park or posted in front of the buildings.

Red had been coming through his hood more frequently lately. He and Indiana had been butting heads and she was starting to get on Red's nerves. It seemed like the more her belly started poking out, the more annoying she became.

Indiana's due date was just around the corner, which Red was happy about. He was ready to finally welcome his baby boy into the world.

Just then his cell phone rang. Red looked at the screen, saw that it was Indiana calling, and swiped to decline the call. As soon as he did, the phone started to ring again. Red couldn't put it off any longer.

"Yo what's good with you ma? Why the fuck you keep blowing up my phone? I'm busy and you keep calling back-to-back!" Red scanned the block as he spoke, seeing Roses walk towards him.

Roses strutted in hot pink booty shorts and a white wife beater, making her look like a full course meal to him.

Indiana's voice woke Red from his wandering thoughts. "I need to have you next to me Red. You know I'm going through it with my emotions. I feel like I'm everywhere right now. I just need some comfort and security."

"Alright then, I'll make it home right after I bust a few moves, ma. I got you. Just fall back and chill out and I'll see you in a few." Red ended the call and looked up at Roses.

"What's poppin blood?" Roses rolled up on Red and threw up the neighborhood handshake with him.

Red's eyes scanned her body, which looked even better up close. His eyes briefly stuttered when he looked at her pelvic area and up top where her cleavage was showing. This particular day Roses was looking extra-good and Red was getting aroused by her. It had been quite some time since Red looked at her in that light. The law of attraction is powerful and most people can't resist it.

"Ain't shit - just out here collecting some paper before I slide back to my crib, ya dig?" Red made eye contact with Roses.

Roses smiled at Red. "You got some bud on you right now? I need to burn something. I ain't smoke in a few days. This nigga I been dealing with is getting on my nerves!" She dug through her purse to get out some money for Red.

Red did a quick survey of his surroundings to see who was paying attention. "Yeah, I got some exotic. Come on - let's roll out to my whip so we can burn one down. It's on me."

Roses followed Red to his cocaine-white BMW X6. "Damn! This your new whip right here? I like this better than that 5 Series you had before." She bent over to examine the new truck up close.

"I like it better too. I guess it was meant to happen when my 5 Series blew up. God seen me in this right here. This is the hoe magnet real talk."

Red smirked as he watched Roses look over his new ride.

They both got in the truck and Red opened up the armrest to get a vanilla Dutch. He grabbed a clear baggie filled with girl scout cookies on Roses' lap. "Go ahead - start breaking up some bud so I can scroll this up blood."

Red began to crack the dutch in half with a razor. He inhaled deep, and realized the smell from Roses' perfume had his nostrils wide open.

When Roses went to put the one-dollar bill on his lap, her knuckle rubbed between his right thigh and his crotch.

Both of them glanced at each other. That simple touch brought back so many memories for them.

Red brushed off his thoughts, quickly rolled up a blunt, and started up the truck so that they could peel off. As he drove down the block, Roses lit up the blunt and inhaled a deep drag. Then she started coughing up a storm.

Red started to laugh as he patted her back. "Damn ma! You got them baby lungs - you can't handle that gas I see." Red took the blunt from her hand and went to put it on his lips. "Damn you were sucking all over the blunt!"

Red wiped off the spit with his fingers before putting it back into his mouth.

Roses looked at Red and licked her succulent lips. "Boy don't act like you never had all this saliva before. Pull over by the park so we can chill instead of driving around risking the police seeing us." Roses pointed at an open parking spot.

Drake's *Landed* started blaring through the speakers just as Roses took the blunt back and started smoking.

"So what's been bracking with your nigga you been dealing with?" Red asked, concerned. "Why is he getting on your nerves? Matter fact, who is ole boy anyway?"

Roses shook her head. "Nah, he be pissing me off with the way he be talking sometimes. The nigga be wild disrespectful. I be tired of it that's all." She quickly added, "You don't know him - he from Jersey," lying through her teeth.

Roses took another pull of the exotic bud. "What's going on with you and your little wifey?"

Right as Red was about to answer her, Roses leaned in and planted a passionate kiss on Red's lips. At first, Red was gonna pull back, but Roses' lips felt so soft and tasted so good that he couldn't resist. After a couple pecks, she slid her tongue inside his mouth.

As they started making out, Red's right hand gently caressed Roses' right breast under her wife beater. The A.C. in the truck had her nipples at full attention. Red pulled her neck back and started to suck and lick it. It had been a while since they had intercourse, but Red always knew all of the hot spots on her body. As Red licked her neck, a loud moan escaped Roses' perfectly shaped lips.

That right there excited Red and drove him to go even further with the foreplay. He let his tongue travel all the way down to her left nipple. Roses immediately got riled up and reached her hands down to grab at his Nike shorts. When she felt his erection, she took control over the entire scenario. Roses unleashed Red's manhood from his boxers and shorts and then leaned over the middle console to devour his swollen member. Her whole mouth made Red's penis disappear instantly.

Red felt the warmth from her mouth and almost busted right there.

He shook off the pleasure from his mind momentarily and focused on lasting so that he could perform. Even though Red couldn't see himself settling down with Roses, he still felt the urge to sex her real good for old times sake.

Roses started deep throating his dick and began to gag. Red watched as his pulsating rod kept sliding in and out of her mouth. Red pulled her head back by her hair, saliva dripping all over her chin and on the driver's seat.

"Yo ma - come ride this dick. I know this is what you really want." Red pointed down, knowing she would jump at the chance to ride him.

Roses hopped over the middle console, sliding off her booty shorts on the way. She gripped the steering wheel with both hands and started riding him, bouncing up and down on his dick. With every stroke, Red gripped her love handles even harder.

"Ohh! Ahh! Ooo!" Roses' moans got louder and louder as Red started to punish her pussy. Her phone kept going off, but they both ignored it.

Roses' tities rubbed against the steering wheel and her head smacked against the windshield because of how fast Red was going at it. The pussy was still just as tight and wet as he remembered it. Red couldn't hold off anymore and exploded right inside her. He tried to pull out, but Roses' weight pressed down on him, making it impossible to do so.

At that very moment, Red knew that he was slipping and got caught up in the hype. Roses was happy that she had gotten what she wanted for a long time. She picked up her booty shorts and slid them back on as she sat back down on the passenger seat.

Red pulled up his Nike shorts and drove back to the hood. On the way back, neither one spoke, clearly afraid of what might come next.

When they got back to the block, something wasn't right. There weren't people standing outside on the stoops, nor were there any kids playing in the streets. Something was wrong.

Red scanned his surroundings and noticed a crowd had formed at the nearby park. He pulled up to the curb, shut off the truck, then jumped out the door, sprinting towards the ruckus. As he approached, he noticed the noise and tension rising.

In the middle of the crowd, B-Money, Deuce Nine, and Klap were beating up an unfamiliar face.

The unknown person's lip was busted, one of his eyes was shut, and they were dogging him pretty bad.

"Hold up, hold up!" Red announced. "Y'all niggas is making the hood hot with this."

The ass-whooping halted immediately, as the bloods noticed who had walked up.

B-Money turned to Red, one hand still on the homie's collar. "Big bro, this nigga right here talking about he claiming Neighborhood Rebels under Bandz!"

Red glared at the kid, menace in his eyes. "Ayo - that Neighborhood Rebel shit you're claiming is a dubb. Point blank, period. Don't scream that no more." He continued to stare down the young homie, stroking his goatee and deep in thought.

"What you trying to do with him?" B-Money asked, keeping a firm grip on ol' boy's shirt.

Red looked around, motioning for the crowd to disperse. He slowly walked up to the boy, close enough so only he could hear his next words.

"Look lil bro, just keep Bandz thinking you're repping his branch off for now, but keep us in tune with his moves and plans. Treason and greed are two things that will get a nigga killed when you playing in the field. So keep this meeting between us right here."

The young homie could see death in Red's eyes, and slowly nodded. He scampered off to his hood as soon as B-Money released him, scared and running for his life.

Red shook his head. Lately his life had been on a roller coaster ride. When everything else seemed to be going right, something else always goes left.

CHAPTER 23

After his conversation with Razor, Diablo knew exactly what he had to do. The blueprint was already on paper from that day forward, as far as Mikey Fingaz was concerned. This wasn't Diablo's first time running the show from inside the pen either.

Being a top-ranked member of the Mexican Mafia made Diablo a very powerful man. He didn't just have power, though. Diablo was always a man of his word and demonstrated that in all of his actions. This was the perfect hit for him: he could keep his word to a friend and also take out a hated enemy at the same time.

Just because he had a life sentence didn't mean he couldn't handle business from the belly of the beast.

Diablo first gave a call to his cousin in Mexico,

explaining the job while the Mexicans watched outside his cell for C.O.'s. He then contacted his nephew in the United States.

Diablo made it perfectly clear the outcome that he desired. If anything else should happen, he would be extremely displeased. And when you pissed off a man like Diablo, you usually ended up dead.

There was no limit as to what Diablo was capable of doing. Once Razor green-lighted his assistance, he would perform just like he said.

It took everything from Razor to agree to give this job away to Diablo, but once he did, he had 100% trust in his ally. Not only was he desperate to get the job done, he needed it done quickly and knew that Diablo was the right man for the job.

As Diablo continued to plan, everything slowly came together over the next few weeks. He knew that even behind bars, his people knew that he always had eyes watching from a distance. No matter where you are or how low you think you are moving, that's just how it is in a gang.

* * *

It was pitch black, and all of Staten Island was fast asleep. The only light shining on Butterworth Avenue was the silver glint from the quarter moon above.

A single black van waited. Inside were two Mexicans who had been waiting for over five hours.

"Come on homes, we have been here waiting so long in this van," Hector said. "Let's come back manana."

Ceza looked at him, then lit up another cigarette. "Homie, ya tu´ sabes. Let's go over the plan one more time."

Ceza leaned over a map of the five-acre property. He pointed out where the other 20 Mexicans were already stationed in place, waiting for their target. He took out the floor plan to the house, once more studying the six bedrooms, four bathrooms, and infinity pool.

"Oye - this cabron definitely knows how to live." Hector whistled as he looked over the expansive property once more.

As the two smoked and laughed, they remembered Diablo's instructions. He had told his two nephews on strict orders not to mess this mission up.

"Let's hurry up and get this done already. I'm tired and ready to get back to my woman." Ceza began to stuff .223 shell casings inside his AK-47 clip. "You know we got a long journey back to Mexico."

Just then, a white Escalade pulled up in the driveway. "Vamanos - show time," Ceza whispered, making the sign of the cross and grabbing his gun.

"Hold on," Hector said, grinning. "Let's give him a minute to get inside and get himself together. I already broke the basement lock for an easy entrance.

Mikey Fingaz got out of his truck and made his way into the estate.

If only he knew that his entire property was surrounded by the most notorious and treacherous ex-military that Mexico had to offer, he might not have left the truck.

The rest of the men waited for the green light from Ceza so they could execute the plan precisely. They waited about half an hour before hearing his voice in their earpieces.

"Dale, dale - now, now!" Ceza yelled, cocking his AK while stepping out of the van.

Mikey Fingaz had no idea what was going on. One thing about being in the streets is that no one is untouchable - especially when they had a bounty on their head.

Ceza and Hector went in through the back of the house, AK-47s trained expertly to cover each other's backs. The other soldiers had already entered the house after disabling the alarm system, and using the latest night vision infared technology and went in search of their prey. Everyone was wearing fatigues, face paint, and was ready to go.

"Lo tenemos - we got him!" Chavez yelled into the earpiece. "We're in the bathroom upstairs."

Ceza had already informed the crew they were not to kill Mikey. This job was personal, and he wanted to look into his eyes before he died.

As Ceza, Hector, and a few others walked upstairs, they heard a commotion from the bathroom. They jogged up the stairs, continuing to train their AK's and sticking to the plan.

When Ceza arrived in the bathroom, he saw four AK-47s pointed at the head of Mikey Fingaz. He lay in the bathtub, smoking on a Cuban cigar while some Tchaikovsky ballet played in the background. He looked calm, even with a bunch of guns pointed at his head. After taking a drag, Mikey scanned each and every face that was packed into his master bathroom.

Mikey realized that not a single face was familiar to him. "So who sent you scumbags into my domain?" He took another puff from the cigar, continuing to act as if he was the king of the world.

"Get the fuck out the bathtub now, cabron!" Ceza yelled. As Mikey slowly stood up, Ceza slapped the cigar from out of his mouth, torpedoing it into the toilet bowl.

Hector saw the speed at which Mikey moved and got impatient. He began slapping him with the butt of his AK in the back of his head repeatedly, leaving a deep gash behind his left ear.

"Ahh hold the fuck up!" Mikey yelled. He dabbed his ear with a towel as he climbed out of the tub.

"Who else is here besides you?" Hector stared into Mikey eyes menacingly.

"Nobody is here. My wife is at her mother's house. If it's money you want, I can get that for you no problem. Just give me a few..."

Mikey didn't even finish his sentence before Ceza punched him in the face. He flew backwards, off balance, and smacked into the bathroom wall.

"Tie him to the shower pole right there," Ceza ordered.

As Hector and one of the other soldiers pulled him up off the floor, Mikey shoved past them and tried to make a run for it. He got about two feet before sliding on a puddle and falling flat on his face. Hector grinned, held him down, and tied his arms to the pole.

Mikey knew he wasn't going to make it out of this alive. His escape attempt didn't work, but he frantically searched the room for another way out. The look on each and every face had murder written all over it.

After Hector finished tying him up, Ceza began punching him in the ribs. He could have easily killed Mikey when they caught him slacking in the bathtub, but that would have been way too easy. Ceza was one of the most treacherous members of the Sinaloa Cartel. He was a fanatic when it came to torturing people. He got a tickle inside watching people beg and plead for their lives.

"Cover his mouth with duct tape," Ceza ordered. As he watched the tape go on, Ceza pulled out a machete from a little black duffle bag he had over his right shoulder.

Mikey Fingaz let out a tiny stream of piss. He knew exactly what was up. This wasn't going to end well for him. He started to panic, and began to scream into the duct tape and squirm to try and escape the tight knots. Unfortunately, the rope was tied too tightly to even think of freedom.

Ceza grabbed Mikey's pinky finger and chopped it off in one swift motion.

Mikey was shocked, and froze for a couple seconds, before writhing in excruciating pain. He looked down at his hand, watching the hot blood gush from the stump where his finger used to be.

"So you're the one who killed my father in California?" Ceza said. "You don't know what you put mi familia through!"

Mikey knew exactly who Ceza was talking about. The reason he moved to Florida and then to New York was to escape the aftermath. The beef had escalated when some Florencia 13 members tried to take over a block, he had invested in. And it just so happened the first person he saw was Diablo's brother Puppet, and slaughtered him.

Hearing Ceza speak brought Mikey back to the murder. He could see the gun in his hand, the bullet through Puppet's head. What brought him back to reality was a machete to his left thumb.

More pain shot through his body. With two fingers missing, Mikey was losing a tremendous amount of blood. He kept trying to break free, but to no avail.

Ceza walked behind Mikey, the machete held expertly in his hand. "Esto es para mi padre, tu´ puta rata." He raised the machete and slit Mikey's throat.

Ceza looked around the bathroom, a gleam of satisfaction and revenge written across his face. For some in his miniature army, this was the first time they had seen him murder. For others, this psychotic side was just another part of him.

Torture was a game that not many killers played. Either their stomach wasn't built for it or they just didn't have the time for it. For Ceza, it was part of what gave him his reputation in Mexico and the states.

As everyone headed downstairs, Ceza stood behind, pulled out his cell phone, and snapped a picture of the body dangling from a rope, blood splattered everywhere.

As he pressed send on his phone, Ceza's voice was barely audible as he said, "Esto es para ti, Diablo." He knew his uncle would be proud of him. The mission was complete.

CHAPTER 24

Every month, Red's community throws a block party for the entire section of the Bronx. Tonight, the block was flooded with all kinds of people from the neighborhood. Red was out as well to show some love and promote unity within the hood. He checked his G-Shock watch, saw it was almost midnight, and took another puff on a blunt of gorilla glue.

Red and his lil homie Klap watched from the stoop of Apple's old building as a few of their younger homies walked to take down the barricades and open the block back up. Just then, a black Yukon Denali sped through the block, eating the stop sign and everything.

Red looked around. There weren't many kids or seniors still outside. Most of the crowd were thots searching for some late-night action and some local hustlers trying to bust a few last licks before they took it inside to the crib. There were only a handful of Neighborhood Gangstas still out there.

The same Yukon Denali came back down the block, this time at a normal speed. Red didn't recognize the truck, and he saw that the Denali's tinted windows still hadn't rolled down as it rolled to a stop right in front of him on the road.

Red's intuition told him something was wrong. He instantly grabbed his .357 chrome Smith & Wesson from his waist. At the same time, the driver's side window slid down.

"Ayo who got some loud fam?" the driver asked. Neither Red nor Klap recognized him.

Klap was thirsty to bust a lick, and ran right up to the truck. "What you needed homie?" He looked down to dig in his pockets. When he looked back up, the barrel of a black .44 Bulldog stared back at him.

Klap put his hands up to swat away the barrel, but he wasn't fast enough. The driver squeezed off three shots at close range.

- BOOM! BOOM! BOOM! -

All three bullets pierced Klap's face, sending a piece of flesh from his cheek flying. He dropped to the ground, limp.

The back window came down, and shots started

flying wildly at Red, who was still standing in front of the building.

Red jumped off the stoop and crouched behind a pile of garbage cans, as others ran around frantically to find similar hiding spots. He drew his .357 and dumped a few shots back, hitting the back driver's side door in the process. He glanced to the sidewalk and saw Klap sprawled out, bleeding profusely.

A few of the Neighborhood Gangstas left outside took out their guns and began shooting at the unknown truck. The driver, hearing all the guns, took the opportunity to drive off.

Red took careful aim and used his last bullet in the chamber to hit one of the shooters right in the neck. The shooter slumped down over the open window, blood splashing over the door of the Yukon as it drove away.

Red popped up and ran towards Klap's lifeless body. "Someone call 911 ASAP!"

He looked around the block for some type of assistance. Klap was one of the up-and-coming Neighborhood Gangstas that Red had gotten attached to.

The sound of sirens closed in on the block from multiple angles. Red passed off his gun to his homie Stay Low. "Blood, put that grip up for me before them people pull up."

Red put both of his hands behind Klap's head,

tilting it so he wouldn't choke on his own blood.

"Red!" A female voice shouted, clearly out of breath.

Red looked up and saw Chantel running towards him.

"Hey Red, I want you to know them dudes that came through here shooting were from 183rd and Davidson. I used to mess with the driver - his name is Hard Body. He just came home like two months ago."

Red scrolled through his mental rolodex. The name sounded so familiar to him, but he just couldn't place it.

As Chantel walked away, it finally clicked. Hard Body was Sha Banga's older brother. He was the big homie for 18 Trey. The name had been on the paperwork from that hood from the state. Red had seen it floating around from his stint at Riker's Island.

Red knew the block would be in a frenzy after the shooting. Everybody loved Red in his hood, so he wasn't worried about anyone snitching. He needed to get away before the police showed up.

Klap's mom pulled up to the sidewalk in a grey sedan. Red looked up, made sure that another homie had Klap, and walked over to her car.

"I will call you later ma to check on your son. I gotta dip before these police ask 100 questions." Red walked back to Klap, pulled out a Ziploc bag filled with weed, winked at Klap's mom, and jogged off towards his BMW.

CHAPTER 25

"My good friend Razor!" Diablo yelled from the top tier. "Come up here to my cell. I would like to speak with you for a minute."

Razor smirked as everyone's eyes followed Diablo's voice, then looked at him. He got up from his plastic T.V. chair and made his way up the stairs. Lately the two of them had been making major moves, which in prison equaled major money. Their bond had grown stronger as time progressed.

Razor walked over to Diablo's cell and stood in the doorway. "What's up homie?"

"Come sit down right here. Let me show you something comrade." Diablo took out a cell phone from a pocket in his pillow and pressed a few buttons. "Check this right here fool!"

Razor sat down and took the offered phone from

Diablo. He looked down and saw Mikey Fingaz hanging from a shower rod, dead.

Razor looked back up at Diablo, wide-eyed. It was rare that you found a real homie outside of your gang, but Razor embraced the opportunity to the fullest.

"Damn homie!" Razor said, pointing at the screen. "You a wild mothafucka. You tripping having that picture up in the phone like that."

"I really don't care. I got forever and a day behind these walls, and the reality is I'm dying in one of these cells." Diablo looked wistful for a moment, and continued. "And to tell you the truth, I'm content with my fate. So that little photo right there is just to show you that I'm a man of my word and our common enemy is where he is where he needs to be: DEAD."

Diablo reached down and grabbed a water bottle. "Take a squirt of this fine white lightning and let's toast to victory!"

* * *

Red had been spending a lot of quality time with Indiana lately. Ever since he had a run-in with the 18 Trey niggas, he fell back from the hood. He was grateful that his little homie Klap had pulled through and survived.

B-Money was running the set for the past two

weeks so that Red could spend more time with Indiana. She was getting closer to her due date and he definitely wanted to welcome his baby boy into this cold world.

The bond that Indiana and Red had created was beyond the average couple's. In Red's mind it was unbreakable. Of course they had trials like any other relationship, but nobody's perfect. That's just how life was designed.

Red leaned over on the couch and kissed Indiana's neck as he rubbed her belly.as the two of them watched 'TV. Red was about to say something, but she cut him off by putting her hand over his mouth and turning up the volume on the news.

"The community on Butterworth Avenue is very nervous and concerned that the killer is still on the loose. This is one of the most gruesome murders that Staten Island has ever seen. We are devastated after the loss of Michael Kujovich, A.K.A. Mikey Fingaz, allegedly a former Russian mob boss. The local police captain vows to make it a top priority to bring closure and justice to this tragedy. Mr. Kujovich was well loved in this community."

Indiana and Red looked at each other in astonishment. Red had no idea what had happened - or why it had happened.

Indiana, on the other hand, knew exactly who had called the hit. She didn't want to tell Red just yet. It might create an unnecessary argument before the baby was born. She made a mental note to send Razor another thousand on his commissary account.

"Damn yo - who killed my opp?" Red mused. "That shit got me all mixed-up." Part of Red felt good that Mikey was gone, but another part felt disappointed that he wasn't the one who killed him.

Red got up from the couch and began pacing back-and-forth in the living room. Indiana sat back and rubbed her belly.

CHAPTER 26

"Yo fool let me go to my cell real quick. I gotta holla at my stepson - he about to have his first baby soon." Razor walked out of Diablo's cell, excited and hopeful that the baby might finally be on the way. As he walked down the stairs, he saw one of his Blood homies Ryder sitting and watching TV by his cell. "Blood, hold me down real quick I gotta use this 9x. You know the lingo if them people coming."

Razor walked inside his cell, grabbed a towel, and hung it over the glass so no one could look inside. He fished out his cell phone, then decided to try Indiana first. She always picked up her phone.

- Ring... Ring... Ring... -

The other line kept ringing, and eventually Indiana's voicemail came on. 'Hmm,' Razor thought to himself. 'I guess I'll try Red then.'

- Ring... Ring... Ring... -

"Damn why the fuck ain't nobody answering their phones?" Razor threw the cell phone down on the bed, agitated.

* * *

"Yo Blood, I need you to pull up on me at my crib ASAP!" Roses said, her voice frantic with worry. "My grandmother ain't breathing and I think she had a heart attack. I just ain't trying to call the police cause I got some shit up here I ain't supposed to have. I already called the ambulance, but I need you here Red. You know I ain't got nobody else to hold me down."

"Alright then, you already know I got you ma," Red replied. "I'm gonna head your way. I'll be there in like 10 minutes cause I ain't that far away." He concentrated on the Bronx traffic ahead of him as he talked on Bluetooth.

Roses quickly glanced at Bandz, who stood next to her. "Okay then Red. See you in a few." She hung up the phone and looked back at Bandz, who glared back. He knew about her and Red.

* * *

Indiana stood up from the couch and headed to the kitchen to grab a snack. On the way, she felt a slight pain in her stomach. She stopped at the kitchen counter, looked down, and saw a huge pool of water grow beneath her.

"Oh my God! The baby is coming!" Indiana quickly called Red's mother to get a ride to the hospital, then called Red.

After two rings, Red answered. "Yo what's good with you ma?"

"Baby my water just broke. I got your mother on her way to drive me to the hospital right now. I'm nervous as hell, so please hurry and make it there. Baby, I need you by my side."

Red knew her well enough to know she was even more nervous than she let on. He also didn't want to let down Roses. He paused for a few seconds in thought.

"Hello baby? You heard me?" Indiana said with an attitude.

"Copy that ma. See you soon, queen."

Red was super excited to get to this point in his life. This moment right here was what turned boys into men. Bringing a child into the world was a blessing from the man above and Red couldn't wait to introduce himself to his son. He had already made a promise to himself that he would be the best possible father.

Traffic eased up ahead, as horns honked and cars sped up. Thank God the next exit was Roses' hood.

* * *

Damn why ain't nobody answering their phones? I'm gonna try my wifey. For real I should have called her first anyway, Razor thought. He called Jennifer, who picked up after only one ring.

"Hey baby, what's up with you? You must have been reading my mind because I was just thinking about you," Jennifer said.

"I tried Red and Indiana, but they didn't pick up. Is everything okay?"

"Yeah - I just emailed you to let you know I'm at the hospital with Indiana. She's going to have her baby!" Jennifer was excited to be a grandmother.

"Well ma that explains where Indiana is at. How about Red?" Razor peeked from behind the towel at the C.O. bubble to make sure he was still in his office. Even though Ryder was the lookout, it didn't hurt to be on point.

"Well Terrell, I don't know where Red is at either. Me and Indiana been trying to get a hold of him for the past hour. I hope he is okay."

"I'm gonna try him one more time," Razor said.

"Oh - and why didn't you tell me you were coming home?" There was a light attitude that crept into Jennifer's voice.

"Baby what are you talking about?" Razor said, confused. "You know something I don't know?"

"Whoop, whoop!" Came from just outside the door.

"Damn baby, I'm gonna have to call you right back. The police coming." He hung up, tucked his cell phone in a compartment, and turned around at the sound of keys jingling.

"Mr Washington!" Someone knocked at the door. "Mr. Washington?" They knocked a second time.

Razor flushed the toilet and opened the door to a half-dozen C.O.s. "What's up with y'all?"

A young, freckled C.O. looked at him. "Mr. Washington, come with us. We need to take you to speak with S.I.S. right now."

* * *

Red pulled up to Roses' hood and called her to let her know to come outside. It went straight to voicemail. He looked around, but didn't see an ambulance in sight.

He drove until he found a parking spot a few houses down from her building on E 174th Street.

It was mid-afternoon in the Bronx River projects, but the block was almost empty.

Red hopped out of the car and spotted a couple of crackheads lingering in front of Roses' building. He tried her cell one more time before heading inside.

- Ring... Ring... -

"Hello?"

"What's poppin blood? Where you at?"

"Come inside the lobby. I'm about to meet you there right now with my grandmother," Roses' voice was trembling.

"Aight bet. I gotta dip after this because my baby mother's water just broke." Red walked towards the building as a teenage boy opened the door for him.

* * *

"Mr. Washington, put your hands on the wall so we can search you." The freckled officer was a rookie, and it looked like he had something to prove. As the C.O.'s hands went towards Razor's waistband, he felt a hard object.

'Shit!' Razor thought. 'I forgot to put my icepick up with the phone!' "Keep your damn hands on that wall! What is this?" The C.O. felt at the object.

Just then, a quick left elbow came crashing

down. Razor wasn't going to go to the SHU just for a knife shot. He was damn well going to make it worthwhile to go to the box.

Four other C.O.s converged on Razor, trying to tackle his 300-lb solid frame to the ground. It wasn't going to be easy. Razor was in the best shape of his life.

Two C.O.s tried to trip him and take him down, but it wasn't working. Another C.O. gave up and sprayed his can of mace in Razor's eyes while a fourth hit his body alarm. All of the police came running to the action in the hallway.

"Get down on the ground now!" A short, chubby officer held a black gun with rubber bullets, aimed directly at Razor.

It took everything inside Razor to raise his hands in the air and get down on his knees to surrender.

* * *

The lobby was empty, except for an old lady getting mail and holding a bag of groceries. Red leaned against a windowsill and started to text Indiana.

The elevator door opened, and Red looked up. Bandz stood there holding a gun.

It took a second for Red to realize what was going on. In that second, Bandz got off two shots at Red, which went into the window behind him.

Red reached for his pistol, but a third shot ripped through the flesh on his right shoulder. The impact knocked him to the floor as another bullet came crashing into his chest.

Bandz walked towards Red on the floor and a young girl walked out of the staircase. The kid started screaming, which startled Bandz. He sent two more shots at Red's motionless body, looked behind him, and ran towards the exit.

When Bandz passed Red's body, he spat on it, then stepped on the screen of his iPhone, smashing it. He flipped up his hoodie, then ran outside.

A small pool of blood grew around Red's body, which laid in the lobby, unmoving.

To be continued...

ABOUT THE AUTHOR

During my current period of confinement in federal prison, I've had the opportunity to master my craft in writing. This was a passageway to escape what was transpiring around me hearing I was so good at expressing myself on paper. I began to take it seriously and practice different writing styles. I also compose music, poems, and I'm even currently designing my own clothing line. I utilized my time to become a positive and productive person.

My first book "Neighborhood Ties", which started out as a web series, eventually unfolded into this masterpiece before you. I let my imagination run wild on this one. I was born and raised in the Bronx of New York City. During my second federal stint I used my time wisely and mastered my writing craft. I invested my time, effort, and energy into something productive. I have learned that what lies before us and what lies behind us are tiny matters compared to what lies within. I'm truly lucky to be alive, but I believe god has me on earth for a bigger purpose. Tune in for my newest projects on Instagram @bigdeal29_ Thank you for all your support.

We Can Help You Self-Publish Your Book
You're The Publisher and We're Your Legs!
We Offer Editing For An Extra Fee, and Highly
Suggest It, If Waved, We Print What You Submit!

We are not your publisher, but we will help you self-publish your own novel.

Ask About our Payment Plans
Contact
Crystal Perkins, MHR
Essence Magazine Bestseller
PO BOX 8044 / Edmond – OK 73083
www.crystellpublications.com
(405) 414-3991

Plan 1-A 190 - 250 pgs. $699.00   Plan 1-B 150 -180 pgs. $674.00
Plan 1-C 70 - 145pgs $625.00

2 (Publisher/Printer) Proofs, Correspondence, 3 books, Manuscript Scan and Conversion, Typeset, Masters, Custom Cover, ISBN, Promo in Mink, 2 issues of Mink Magazine, Consultation, POD uploads. 1 Week of E-blast to a reading population of over 5000 readers, book clubs, and bookstores, The Authors Guide to Understanding The POD, and writing Tips, and a review snippet along with a professional query letter will be sent to our top 4 distributors in an attempt to have your book shelved in their bookstores or distributed to potential book vendors. After the query is sent, if interested in your book, distributors will contact you or your outside rep to discuss shipment of books, and fees.

Plan 2-A 190 - 250 pgs. $645.00   Plan 2-B 150 -180 pgs. $600.00
Plan 2-C 70 - 145pgs $550.00

1 Printer Proof, Correspondence, 3 books, Manuscript Scan and Conversion, Typeset, Masters, Custom Cover, ISBN, Promo in Mink, 1 issue of Mink Magazine, Consultation, POD upload.

Made in United States
Orlando, FL
25 April 2023